Look Out Below!

JUL 12

Frank polished off a cracker and washed it down with a swig from his canteen. "Well, looks like it's time to hit the road again."

"Hey!" said a voice from above. "You really can see water of some sort."

Frank, Chet, Joe, and Phil turned to see Biff hanging from a tree limb.

"I'll be down in a minute," Biff said. "Great view up here. If I move a little farther out on the limb, I might be able to see all the way back to Bayport."

"That's highly unlikely," Phil replied. "Bayport's too far over the horizon. Maybe you could see all the way to—"

A loud snapping sound interrupted Phil. Biff had shinnied out to the far end of the tree branch, his legs and arms wrapped around it.

Stunned, they all watched as the branch split in two and Biff plummeted twenty feet to the ground!

The Hardy Boys
Mystery Stories

**Available from MINSTREL Books
and ALADDIN Paperbacks**

THE **HARDY BOYS**®

#162
THE END OF THE TRAIL

FRANKLIN W. DIXON

Aladdin Paperbacks
New York London Toronto Sydney Singapore

First Aladdin Paperbacks edition August 2002
First Minstrel edition July 2000

Copyright © 2000 by Simon & Schuster, Inc.

ALADDIN PAPERBACKS
An imprint of Simon & Schuster
Children's Publishing Division
1230 Avenue of the Americas
New York, NY 10020

Printed in the United States of America.

20 19 18 17 16 15 14 13

THE HARDY BOYS and THE HARDY BOYS MYSTERY
STORIES are trademarks of Simon & Schuster, Inc.

ISBN-13: 978-0-671-04759-7
ISBN-10: 0-671-04759-0
0312 OFF

Contents

THE END OF THE TRAIL

1 On the Appalachian Trail

"I can see the ocean from here!" Joe Hardy shouted excitedly.

He was hanging from the lowest branch of a towering pine tree, on top of an even more towering mountain in the Appalachian range. A beautiful summer sky arched above him as the sun rose above the horizon.

"That's impossible!" Phil Cohen shouted up at him from twenty feet below. "The ocean's more than a hundred miles away! You must be seeing a lake!"

"If you break your neck, I'm going to ask Dad if I can have your room," Joe's brother, Frank, yelled, staring up at him along with Phil, Chet Morton, and Biff Hooper.

"Oh, relax," Joe said. "Hanging from this limb is no

worse than doing the parallel bars in gym class. I could hang here all day."

Frank smiled and ran his fingers through his dark brown hair. Frank, at eighteen, was a year older than Joe, and sometimes his younger brother drove him a little crazy. When they and their three friends had set out on this 250-mile hike along the Appalachian Trail, he had promised his father, Fenton Hardy, that he would get everybody through in one piece. Joe was doing his best to thwart Frank's plan.

"Maybe," Frank said slyly, "the rest of us will eat breakfast while you're up there. Won't be much food left when you get back down."

"All right!" Chet exclaimed, raising his eyes from the hand-held game machine where he was playing a game called Bear Hunter. "I thought we'd *never* eat!"

"Why do you keep playing a game about hunting bears in the woods?" Biff asked. "You really *are* in the woods. And you really could bump into a bear or two."

"Somehow the game is more fun," Chet said, not looking up. "If I get eaten by a bear in this game, at least I can hit Start and play again. But if I get eaten by a bear along the trail . . ."

"Some lucky bear will have the best meal of its life," Frank said, gazing at Chet's ample girth.

Joe began working his way along the limb, back

toward the tree trunk. "You guys are not going to eat breakfast without me."

Frank smiled. Joe knew that he was being tricked into climbing back down, but Chet alone could finish off their daily breakfast ration in five minutes. Chet was known for his voracious appetite, and it was dangerous to leave food unattended when Chet was hungry—which he almost always was.

Biff, who looked like a weight lifter and wasn't bothered by the task of lugging seventy-five pounds of gear up mountains, grabbed the backpack full of food that was lying next to his sleeping bag. "Okay, I've got the food. Someone divvy it up."

"I will," Chet said.

"Huh-uh," Frank said. "I'll divide up the food. Last time I let you do it, you ate all the beef jerky."

"That was an accident," Chet protested.

Joe came rushing up, his T-shirt and blue jeans covered with bark and pine needles from the tree he had just climbed down. "Here I am. Nothing like a refreshing climb after spending the night in the woods. So, did you save anything for me?"

"A drumstick, stuffing, and pumpkin pie," Frank said. "Knock yourself out."

The quintet of teenagers looked down at their meal. Frank had laid out two tins of sardines, five whole grain crackers, and five canteens of water.

"Sardines again?" Chet moaned. "We've had the

same thing since we started hiking a week ago. Couldn't you at least open *another* tin of sardines? I'm starving to death."

"We agreed when we set out that we'd have sardines for breakfast," Frank said.

"And trail mix for lunch," Joe said.

"And jerky for dinner," Biff added. "I'm sick of jerky."

"Hey," Frank said to Biff. "If you want to carry a pack filled with two weeks' worth of gourmet meals, we'll stop off at the next grocery store."

"Er, no thanks," Biff said. "Even the sardine cans are too heavy."

Joe sat down and pulled a small tin plate out of his pack. He piled three sardines on it and began to eat.

"Remind me again why we're here," he said. "I'm having trouble remembering."

Phil Cohen popped a sardine in his mouth and stared off wistfully into the trees. "Because we wanted to hike the Appalachian Trail," he said. "The largest supervised wilderness trail on the East Coast of the United States. Begun in 1921 and completed in 1937."

"Oh, yeah," Joe said. "It was *your* idea. Remind me to put a snake in your sleeping bag tonight."

Chet stuffed three sardines into his mouth at once. "I wonder what a snake would taste like?" he said, gazing at his empty plate as though he expected to find more sardines on it.

"Probably like chicken," Frank said.

"We have chicken?" Chet said, too busy swallowing to catch every word Frank said. "Have you been holding out on me?"

Frank rolled his eyes. "No, we don't have chicken. Or chalupas. Or quarter-pound burgers. Or Starvin' Guy microwave dinners. Or any of the other things you've been asking for all week."

"Boy, I wish we had a microwave," Chet said. "And something to put in it."

Joe polished off his last sardine and leaned back on his elbows. "So, Phil, to get us going tell us one more time why the Appalachian Trail is so cool."

Phil Cohen's face brightened. He loved sharing his vast knowledge. "There are so many reasons," he said excitedly.

"Which you've told us two hundred times, at least," Chet said under his breath.

"The Appalachian Trail stretches from Georgia to Maine," Phil continued.

"So does Route 95," Joe said. "And it starts in Florida."

"The Appalachian Trail follows the crest of the Appalachian Mountains," Phil continued.

"Which must be why my legs are so sore," Frank said.

"There are more than forty thousand different species of insects along the trail," Phil said.

Biff picked at a sardine. "I think this is one," he said, holding up a finger with a black dot on it.

"Ewwwww," Chet said. "You mean there are insects on our food?"

"Don't worry, Chet," Frank said. "Insects are protein, like hot dogs."

"Really?" Chet asked.

"Yeah," Joe said. "We'll have Aunt Gertrude bake us a cockroach casserole when we get home."

"And finally," Phil said, slightly annoyed at the interruption, "the Appalachian Trail is something that everybody should experience. The American wilderness is vanishing rapidly, and we're lucky that we still have a chance to explore it."

"Let's have a big round of 'America the Beautiful,'" Frank said. "'O beautiful for spacious skies . . .'"

"Can't we sing something a little newer?" Biff asked.

"Do you know any other songs about 'purple mountain majesties'?" Frank asked. He waved at the view behind the group. Just visible through the trees was another mountain range, grayish blue in the morning sun. "We've got our own purple mountain majesties. Looks pretty good."

"I want a better look," Biff said, springing to his feet. "I'm going to climb Joe's tree."

"We have to get moving soon," Frank said. "We've got a schedule to keep." He was too late. Biff was on his way to the tree Joe had been hanging from just minutes earlier.

Frank polished off a cracker and washed it down with a swig from his canteen. "Well, looks like it's time to hit the road again."

"So soon?" Chet said. "Hey, how about a second helping of sardines?"

"If we take a second helping," Joe said, rising from his sitting position and stretching his arms, "we'll be out of food before we get to the end of the trail."

"Hey!" said a voice from far above. "You really can see water of some sort from here."

All heads turned to see Biff hanging from Joe's tree limb.

"Okay, Biff," Frank said. "Come on down. We've got some hiking to do."

"I'll be down in a minute," Biff said. "Great view up here. If I move a little farther out on the limb, I might be able to see all the way back to Bayport."

"That's highly unlikely," Phil replied. "Bayport's too far over the horizon. Maybe you could see all the way to—"

A loud snapping sound interrupted Phil. Biff had shinnied out to the far end of the tree branch, his legs and arms wrapped around it.

Stunned, they all watched as the branch split in two and Biff plummeted twenty feet to the ground!

2 Morgan's Quarry

"Biff!" Joe cried, rushing forward. But he was too late. Biff hit the ground with his knees and crumpled into a heap.

Frank ran up to where his friend lay. Biff wasn't moving. He seemed to be unconscious.

"He's hurt," Frank said. "Let's check him out, Joe."

Joe crouched next to Biff and gently lifted his wrist, placing his thumb on Biff's pulse.

Biff moaned. "Hey, what're you doing? Let go of my hand."

"Glad to see you're alive," Frank said.

"Yeah, I'm alive," Biff said. "Why shouldn't I be? The last thing I remember was . . . I was looking at a great view. What happened?"

"You fell out of the tree," Chet told him.

"No wonder I feel so awful," Biff said, putting a hand on his head. "How did I get this headache?"

"Could be a concussion," Frank said. "We'd better get you to a hospital."

Joe leaned over and stared deeply into Biff's eyes.

"Hey, what are you doing?" Biff said. "Stop looking at me like that."

"I'm checking your eyes to see if you have a concussion, Biff," Joe said. "Your pupils are the same size and don't appear to be dilated. I think you're okay."

"Hey, I'm terrific," Biff said. "I work out every day. A little fall out of a tree isn't going to hurt me."

"That wasn't exactly a *little* fall," Joe said. "You fell twenty feet. You could have been killed."

"I'm made of iron," Biff said. "Just give me a hand to help me stand up."

"If you're made out of iron," Frank said, "how come you need help standing up?"

Frank held out his hand. Biff grabbed it and began pulling himself up. Suddenly he screamed in pain and fell back.

"Yow!" Biff exclaimed. "I think I broke my leg."

"Oh, great," Joe said. "You're injured and we're out here in the middle of nowhere."

"Does this mean I can have his sardines?" Chet asked, trying to lighten the mood.

9

"No," Frank said firmly. "It means Biff will probably get *your* sardines. And we have got to get Biff to a doctor—fast."

"A doctor?" Joe asked. "Then we'll need to locate the nearest town."

Phil grabbed his backpack and opened a flap. "I've got the map right here. We'll find a town and carry Biff there."

"Carry Biff?" Chet said jokingly. "How much do you weigh, Biff?"

"Never mind that," Joe said. "We'll carry him together. We can make a travois out of some tree branches and those bungie cords we brought with us."

"A travois?" Chet asked.

"It's kind of a like a stretcher," Frank said. "Native Americans used them for transporting food."

"Here it is," Phil said, stabbing a finger at the map. "There's a town called Morgan's Quarry that can't be too far from here. I'd say it's about ten miles away."

"Ten miles?" Frank said. "We won't get there until afternoon."

"Well," Phil said, "the second nearest town is Brighton, which is about seventy-five miles away."

"On second thought," Frank said, "maybe Morgan's Quarry isn't so far away after all. How do we get there?"

"There's a side path about two or three miles

from here," Phil said. "We head straight down it and we'll end up on the east edge of Morgan's Quarry."

"Okay," Frank said. "Let's make that travois and get moving."

Biff made a sour face, but it was clear that he wasn't going to be walking for a while. Joe and Chet gathered branches while Phil and Frank pulled the cords from their backpacks. First they placed two bundles of branches side by side and laced the cords between them, strapping them tightly to the branches at both ends. Then Frank and Joe grabbed Biff by the shoulders and midsection and laid him on top of the contraption.

"Hey, guys, take it easy," Biff complained. "You aren't carrying food on this thing!"

"Be careful with his leg," Frank told Joe. "It might hurt when we set it down."

"Cool," Joe said. "Maybe we can break a few extra bones for good measure."

"Very funny," Biff said, but he lay still as the two brothers gently made him comfortable on the makeshift stretcher.

"Done," Frank said. "Now let's drag and carry him to, um . . ."

"Morgan's Quarry," Phil answered.

"Yeah, that's the place," Frank said. He lifted one pole of the travois, and Joe took the other. Together they would pull Biff on the travois while Chet and

Phil walked beside it to protect Biff from branches and rocks. Chet and Phil would take the second shift at pulling.

The four friends began hiking along the trail, backpacks strapped to their shoulders, Biff's strapped to the travois. For the last week they had moved briskly along the tops of mountains, but now every step had to be made cautiously. They had to protect Biff as the trail went downhill, then back up. The ground underneath had been cleared by the feet of thousands of hikers, but all of a sudden it seemed very rough.

"There's the path that will lead off to Morgan's Quarry!" Phil cried, pointing between two trees.

"How can you tell?" Joe asked. "Just looks like more bushes to me."

"There's a blue blaze on that tree," Phil said. "Look."

Joe stared at the tree. There was a small slash of blue paint on one side.

"So there is," Joe said. "I should have paid closer attention. Guess I'm worried about Biff."

The four hikers maneuvered Biff to the edge of the trees. They could just make out a narrow footpath winding between the undergrowth.

"The 'road' to Morgan's Quarry," Frank said.

They moved into the trees, following the path. All at once it became darker, as if the sun were about to set. Only a small amount of light trickled past the leaves and thick branches above.

"I wish they had streetlights along here," Chet said.

"This is a wilderness area," Phil snapped. "There aren't any streetlights. Or fast-food restaurants. Or gas stations. That's the whole point."

"Ooh, why did you mention that? I sure wish there was a fast-food restaurant," Chet said. "I could go for a triple cheeseburger with onions and special sauce right about now."

"Oh, yeah," Joe said. "They'd get lots of customers out here. Mostly bears."

"Did you see a bear?" Chet asked, concern darkening his face.

"You've been playing your video game too long," Joe said.

The path began slanting downhill even steeper, leading into a valley far below. Birds twittered in the trees, jumping from branch to branch.

"Boy," Joe said. "Ten miles isn't far when you're in a car, but when you're dragging a big guy like Biff it might as well be a hundred miles."

"Hey, Biff," Joe said. "Maybe you could hop along on your good leg. Sure would make life easier."

"I'd love to," Biff said, lifting himself with his arms. "But I don't think I'd make a very convincing Easter Bunny."

"I don't know," Frank said. "I'd pay a lot to see you as the Easter Bunny."

"Don't hold your breath waiting," Biff said, easing himself back down.

After a few hours the path widened as they reached the bottom of the hill. Where before the hikers had had to maneuver around trees and bushes, now they had an open, well-trod path.

"We must be near the town," Frank said.

"If we're not near the town," Joe said, "I say we leave Biff behind. Maybe somebody else will find him."

"Somebody a lot nicer than you guys," Biff complained with a grin.

"Hey, looks like civilization up ahead!" Joe cried.

Sure enough, a wooden building was barely visible through the trees. As the teens continued down the path, more buildings appeared.

"Morgan's Quarry," Frank said. "At last."

Joe groaned. "Not a second too soon. I think Biff's put on at least a hundred pounds since we left the trail."

"It could be worse," Biff said. "You could be carrying Chet."

"Hey, what do you mean by that?" Chet exclaimed.

The path abruptly ended, opening into a grassy field surrounded by the buildings that had been visible a moment earlier. A wooden sign read Welcome to Morgan's Quarry.

"Looks like we're here," Frank said. "Wherever here is."

"It's pretty obvious they won't have a hospital," Joe said. "The town looks pretty small. And pretty old."

"They won't have a hospital," Phil said, "but they may have a doctor."

"Well, let's find somebody and ask where the doctor might be," Frank suggested.

Finding somebody wasn't going to be easy. The wooden buildings were old houses and most appeared deserted. Paint was flaking off the walls, and the windows were cracked.

"It's a ghost town," Frank said. "I bet everybody left years ago."

"I would have," Chet said. "There probably isn't even a decent grocery store."

"Not so fast," Frank said. "Looks like the place is populated after all."

About a hundred feet to the side of them the hikers could see two men walking and carrying a large sack between them. The two men were in their twenties, thin but wiry looking, with unshaven faces and long hair. They didn't seem to notice the five strangers who had just emerged from the woods.

"Hey!" Joe shouted. "Can you guys help us?"

One of the men turned abruptly, startled. He dropped his end of the bag, which broke open, spilling the contents onto the ground.

"Sorry about that," Frank said, moving closer to the men. "We just wanted to ask you for directions."

15

The man didn't reply. He stared angrily at the hikers, then glanced down at what had spilled on the ground.

Frank, Joe, Phil, and Chet also glanced at the ground. What had spilled out of the bag was a huge pile of money.

3 Vietnam Revisited

The teens stared with their mouths hanging open. The two men stared back, surly expressions on their faces. An awkward silence hung between the two groups.

"Er, can we help you with that?" Frank asked, not sure what to do or say.

"Stay away," growled the man who had dropped the bag. "What are you kids doing here?"

"We just came off the Appalachian Trail," Joe said.

"Well, get back on it—right now," the man said.

"We can't," Frank said. "Our friend is hurt. He may have broken a leg."

"Go see Doc Harrison," the man said, waving toward a wooden building. "And leave us alone."

"Thanks," Joe said. "I think." He gave Frank an odd look. "Seems there *is* a doc in town."

With Biff securely attached to the travois, the four hikers began making their way between two of the wooden buildings. On the other side was a crudely paved street, with a sign that read Main Street. Along Main Street was a genuine town, though it looked like something left over from an earlier time. Main Street was lined on either side with buildings, including a general store with a large wooden sign proclaiming it as Sugaree's Shack. At one end the street branched off in two directions, one going toward a hill atop which the hikers could just make out what appeared to be a large mansion, the other toward some distant woods. In the other direction it vanished around a curve. As they walked along the street, Chet spotted a sign on the front of an old house.

"Look!" Chet cried. "That sign says, Rhonda Harrison, RN."

"A registered nurse," Frank said thoughtfully.

"A nurse isn't a doctor," Biff said, concern raising the pitch of his voice.

"Beggars can't be choosers," Joe said.

"A nurse can help you with that leg," Frank said. "Let's see if Rhonda can fit you into her schedule."

Joe pushed the doorbell. An old-fashioned chiming noise came from inside.

"At least the doorbell works," Joe said. "Maybe this town hasn't completely fallen apart."

18

There was silence inside for a moment, then the sound of footsteps. The door cracked open.

A woman peered out. She was middle-aged, with graying long brown hair that appeared to be uncombed. She wore an exercise suit, and her face was covered with sweat, as though she had been working out. Her eyes were suspicious but not unfriendly.

"Can I help you?" she asked.

"Our friend here may have broken his leg," Joe said.

The nurse looked down at Biff, concern clouding her features.

"Let me have a look." She opened the door all the way. "Bring him into the house."

"Thanks," Frank said.

The hikers carried Biff into a large living room. The furniture was old and thickly padded, Frank noticed, but it was well kept. The pine-scented air freshener was not successfully masking a musty smell of mildew.

"My name is Rhonda, by the way," the woman said. "Rhonda Harrison. I'm a nurse."

"Where should we put Biff?" Frank asked.

"Right here, on the sofa," Rhonda said. "I need to examine him."

Chet and Phil stepped aside as Frank and Joe laid Biff gently on the overstuffed sofa.

"Ow!" Biff yelled. "Did you have to drop me like that?"

"We didn't drop you," Joe said. "We put you down like a teacup."

"Yeah, well, I think you just broke this teacup into a million pieces," Biff groaned.

"You're okay, Biff," Rhonda said. "I'll take care of you now."

"Better than letting those guys take care of me," Biff snapped.

Rhonda crouched beside the sofa. With Frank's help, she removed his hiking boots and socks. Because he had on shorts, she didn't have to remove his pants.

"Do you feel anything when I do this?" Rhonda asked, squeezing Biff's toes.

"Yeooowwwww!" Biff screeched. "Yeah, it feels like you're hammering nails in my leg."

"Good," Rhonda said. "That means there's no nerve damage. What happened to you, anyway?"

"He fell out of a tree," Chet said.

"From twenty feet up," Joe added.

Rhonda looked at Biff reprovingly. "You're lucky to be alive."

"Well, it hurts," Biff said.

"Being alive hurts," Rhonda said. "We'll get you fixed up. Don't worry."

"So what's wrong with him?" Phil asked.

Rhonda ran her hand gently along Biff's leg. "He doesn't seem to have any major injuries, amazingly enough."

"So we can hit the trail again?" Joe asked.

"Not any time soon," Rhonda said. "I'm just about positive your friend Biff has a break, up near the knee. And a serious muscle sprain. There's a bit of swelling around the knee. I want to set his leg to keep it from moving. I don't think he needs a hospital. They could x-ray the leg, but I think that would just confirm what I'm pretty positive about the leg—it's broken. I think it's better if he just rests here for a bit. He's been pretty traumatized."

"Does that mean we'll have to hang out here for a while?" Chet asked.

"For a couple of days," Rhonda said. "Then it should be safe to move him."

"Are you sure he can't be moved now?" Joe asked. "Once you've got his leg immobilized, we could get him to a bigger town." He raised an eyebrow at his brother, questioning Rhonda's decision. Frank shrugged back.

"I don't recommend it," Rhonda said decisively, ending all discussion.

"Do you know a good restaurant?" Chet asked, changing the subject to one of his favorites.

"Or a place to pitch our sleeping bags?" Frank asked.

"You don't need to sleep out," Rhonda said. "Mrs. Hibley, next door, has a boardinghouse. I'm sure she'd be glad to put you up—and feed you," she added for Chet's benefit. "Only ten dollars a night."

"Good thing we brought some cash," Joe said. "I never thought we'd really need it on the trail."

"Where will *I* spend the night?" Biff asked.

"I've got a guest room," Rhonda said. "I use it for patients. I keep my supplies there. Believe it or not, the people in this town occasionally get sick."

"Do you need us to move him in there?" Frank asked.

"I'd appreciate it," Rhonda said, pointing toward a back room. Frank and Joe began to lift Biff.

"Not again!" Biff complained. "Don't leave any bruises this time, okay?"

The brothers carried him through the door. A large bed filled much of the room. Frank and Joe laid Biff on top of a thick down comforter.

"Nice place," Chet said. "I wouldn't mind spending the night here myself."

"Break a leg and you'll be welcome," Rhonda said.

"Uh, no, thanks," Chet replied.

"Now let's get down to business," Rhonda said to Biff.

Biff's expression mirrored his fear.

"Don't worry," Rhonda said. "I'm not doing surgery. But I have to immobilize your leg."

"Okay," Biff said. "Just keep any knives away from me."

Rhonda smiled and kiddingly held up a sharp scalpel

with an evil glint in her eyes. She put the scalpel down and examined his leg again. His knee was puffy and dark red. There were several bright red lacerations on his calf, some of which appeared to be infected.

"Ewwww," Biff said. "It feels like something's about to come bursting out of my leg like in an *Alien* movie."

"Probably something green and hungry," Joe said. "Like Chet."

Chet gave Joe a dirty look. "I'm not green. . . ."

"Okay, you guys, give Biff a break," Rhonda said.

"Hey, I can take it," Biff declared. "I give back as good as I get."

"Lie down, Biff," Rhonda said. "I'm going to clean your wounds, then prepare your plaster. This will take about half an hour, and you'll need to lie still for a while to let the plaster set."

"Why not just use one of those Velcro splints?" Frank asked. "That would be a lot easier."

"I don't have any more," Rhonda said. "I don't have access to a continuous supply of medical paraphernalia out here in the woods."

"This is great," Joe said. "We'll be laid up in this town for days before Biff heals."

"Not that long," Rhonda said. "We'll get Biff moved soon enough."

"There go our plans for hiking another hundred miles on the trail," Frank said.

Rhonda gave Frank a stern look. "I don't think you

23

want to go without your friend. And you can always come back sometime later to finish your hike."

"Sorry," Frank said guiltily. "If Biff needs time to heal, we'll stick around, of course."

Rhonda opened a cabinet next to the bed and pulled out several rolls of surgical tape. She laid the tape next to Biff and began wrapping it around his leg. Biff's face contorted with pain, but he remained silent.

"So," Chet asked. "How did you become a nurse?"

Rhonda pulled another layer of tape around Biff's leg with a twist of her arm. "In Vietnam," she said matter-of-factly.

Biff's eye's fluttered open, despite his pained expression. "Vietnam? You were in 'Nam?"

"Yeah," Rhonda said. "From '67 through '69. I worked at a Mobile Surgical Unit near Da Nang."

"Wow!" Chet said. "A MASH unit. Like on that old TV show."

"It wasn't much like TV," Rhonda said. "It was mostly boring—until they'd bring in a helicopter filled with guys who had been shot full of bullets or who had stepped on land mines. A lot of the soldiers didn't live to get home. But we did our best to keep them alive."

"I'm sure you did," Joe said, not knowing what else to say.

"The Vietnam War was fought mostly in jungles, with snipers waiting to shoot you when you didn't expect it," Rhonda continued. "I know guys who still can't sleep because they're worried that somebody's hiding around the corner to kill them. They don't like to remember what happened. A lot of them saw their best friends get killed."

"I can't imagine going through that," Joe said.

Rhonda looked up from the bandage that she was wrapping around Biff's leg. "Be grateful that you don't have to. I lost some friends over there. Some really close friends."

"Did you have a boyfriend over there?" Phil asked.

"A husband," Rhonda said. "I really don't want to talk about it."

Silence fell over the room. Finally Biff said, "While I'm here, maybe you can tell me some of what you saw."

"Maybe," Rhonda said. She stood up and walked to the cabinet, where she removed a plaster kit to apply to the bandages she had just wrapped around Biff's leg.

A smile creased Rhonda's face. "I haven't told my stories in a long time. Maybe it'll be good—for me, too."

"It must be pretty painful to recall some of it," Frank said.

"You can't imagine," Rhonda said, rubbing plaster over Biff's bandages. "Nobody can imagine."

Frank cleared his throat. "Maybe we should have a

look around the town while Rhonda fixes Biff up."

"What town?" Chet asked. "I didn't see anything outside except a few old buildings."

"There was that general store across the street," Joe said. "Sugar's Shack or something like that."

"And we need to find a room at Mrs. Hibley's, next door," Phil said.

"Then let's go," Frank said. "You'll be okay, Biff?"

Biff smiled gamely as Rhonda slapped plaster onto his leg. "Yeah, I'll be fine."

"Actually, this really would be a good time for you to get out and take a look around Morgan's Quarry," Rhonda said.

"Okay, everybody," Frank said. "Let's clear out."

Frank, Joe, Chet, and Phil left the guest room and headed across the living room to the front door. Outside, it was still daylight, though Main Street was deserted.

The sign that proclaimed Sugaree's Shack was directly across the street. It looked as though it had been painted many years ago, though the picture of a smiling woman's face next to the name looked as if it had been done by a talented artist. Beside the crumbling wooden buildings, the sign seemed almost out of place.

"Let's take a look over there first," Frank said. "Then we'll get a room."

Frank pushed open the door to Sugaree's Shack. Inside was an old-fashioned general store, with unpainted wooden shelves and a large counter in the rear. The shelves were poorly stocked, but a few items of food and a couple of tools were available. Behind the counter, a young woman in her late teens looked up expectantly. She had blond hair that reached to her shoulders and bright eyes. She seemed particularly interested in Frank.

"Can I help you?" she asked.

"Well, maybe," Frank asked. "We're new to town."

"I figured that," the girl said. "We don't get a lot of strangers here."

"Not a lot of locals either, I'd bet," Joe said. "This town doesn't seem to have a very large population."

"It used to be bigger," the girl said. "My name's Loraleigh. Like Laura Lee but spelled L-O-R-A-L-E-I-G-H. Loraleigh Mason. Do you guys have names?"

"Well, that's Frank," Joe said, pointing at his brother. "And I'm Joe. And this is Chet and Phil."

"Glad to meet you," Phil said.

"Likewise," Chet said. "Is that beef jerky on the shelf over there?"

"Yes, it is," Loraleigh said. "We've got lots of jerky. It keeps forever."

"Yeah, that's why we brought it along for dinner," Joe said. "Every night. All jerky, all the time."

Loraleigh's face darkened. "I've heard about you guys," she said.

"Huh?" Joe said. "We just got here."

"What did you hear?" Frank asked.

"I can't tell you," Loraleigh said. "You don't want to know."

"Yes, we do," Joe insisted. "Tell us."

"Okay," she said, meeting Joe's steady gaze. "I've heard that you're in a lot of trouble."

"Trouble?" asked Frank.

"That's right," Loraleigh said. "And if you don't get out of this town right away, you could be in *big* trouble."

4 No Exit

Frank stared at Loraleigh in astonishment. "In trouble? Why?"

"Yeah, why?" Joe said. "Usually nobody hates us until we've poked our noses into a few places where we don't belong."

"Tell us more," Frank said.

Loraleigh shrugged. "I can't tell you any more than what I've said."

"That's not fair," Chet said. "You can't tell us something like that and then leave us hanging."

Loraleigh ignored them and pulled a small cardboard box down from a shelf behind the counter.

"Would you like some mints?" she asked, holding the box out to the Hardys and their friends. "We have the chocolate-covered kind."

"All right!" Chet exclaimed, his face breaking out in a radiant smile. "I love mints. I'll take one package."

"Great," Joe said. "She's already distracted Chet with food."

Frank leaned across the counter. "Okay, you don't want to tell us why we're in trouble. But at least you can tell us about this store—and your town."

"I might be able to do that," Loraleigh said. "What do you want to know?"

"Well, why is the town called Morgan's Quarry?" Phil asked.

"Because there's a large granite quarry about two miles from here," Loraleigh said. "The town was built around the quarry. The whole McSavage Corporation was built around the quarry. They had a major mining operation here for years, which they bought back around 1900 from a guy whose family started it. Their name was Morgan."

"The McSavage Corporation?" Joe asked.

"Owned by the McSavage family," Loraleigh told them. "The last McSavage owns that big house up on the hill. Maybe you noticed it."

"As a matter of fact," Frank said, "I noticed a mansion on a hill when we came into town."

"That's it—the McSavage mansion," Loraleigh said. "He owns the quarry."

"I bet he's rich," Chet said.

"Not exactly rich anymore, but okay," Loraleigh said. "All of the granite was dug out of the quarry by the 1920s."

"And the quarry was the only source of income for this town?" Frank asked.

"Pretty much," Loraleigh said.

"So how has the town survived without the quarry?" Joe asked.

"Not well, but we make do," Loraleigh said with a shrug.

"I'm not sure it *has* survived," Phil said. "The population of the town appears to be small; the houses are neglected; you don't have much stuff on the shelves. I'd say that this town is pretty much dead now that the quarry is gone."

"Like I said," Loraleigh told Phil, her brow furrowed, "we make do."

"Okay," Frank said. "I've got another question. Why is this store called Sugaree's Shack?"

Loraleigh's face brightened. "Sugaree was my great-great-great-grandmother. She was a young southern woman who moved north after the Civil War. She opened this store to sell groceries and tools to miners."

Joe glanced around at the dusty shelves. "This place kind of looks like it's left over from just after the Civil War."

"Actually," Loraleigh said, "it was rebuilt in the 1920s."

"Was anything in this town built after the 1920s?" Frank asked.

"Not much," Loraleigh told him. "Like I said, the mine ran out of granite. There hasn't been much money in town since then."

Joe patted his pocket. "Hey, maybe I'm the richest guy around. Want to sell me some of your most expensive goodies?"

"The richest guy in town, although not that rich," Loraleigh informed him, "is Bill McSavage, the one who lives in that mansion on top of the hill."

"How has the McSavage family managed to keep some of its money if they haven't had a granite quarry since the 1920s?" Chet asked.

"They made some good investments," Loraleigh said. "Now, can I sell you something?"

"I'd like this compass," Phil said, pulling a box off one of the shelves. "It's nicer than the one I brought along."

"And I'd like this jerky," Chet said, carrying two cartons over to the counter.

"Think that's enough to hold you?" Joe asked.

"I'm not sure," Chet said. "Maybe I should get more."

"I'll take this map," Frank said, pulling a folded piece of paper from a stack at the edge of the counter. "It's a map of this town, right?"

"That's right," Loraleigh said. "Of course, that map was made in 1924."

"That's okay," Frank said. "Looks like nothing has changed much since then."

"I was born after that," Loraleigh said flirtatiously, staring Frank directly in the eye.

"That's true," Frank said with an embarrassed grin. "I guess that was a pretty important event."

"My parents thought so," Loraleigh said.

"Are you from around here?" Joe asked.

"Sure am," Loraleigh said. "My house is three doors down, where the road forks toward the McSavage family mansion. I live with my father. He owns this store. My mother died a couple of years ago."

"I'm sorry," Frank said.

"Thanks," Loraleigh said. "But accidents happen. She liked to ride horses and was thrown by her favorite. Doc Harrison tried to save her, but she couldn't do it."

"Doc Harrison," Chet repeated. "You mean Rhonda?"

"That's right," Loraleigh said. "You've met her?"

"She's taking care of our friend Biff," Joe said.

"Your friend couldn't be in better hands," Loraleigh said. "Doc Harrison has been taking care of people in this town since the early seventies."

"When she came back from Vietnam?" Frank asked.

"That's right," Loraleigh said. "Rhonda grew up in this town and came back as soon as she finished her

33

tour of duty. Everybody was very proud of her. Of course, I wasn't around then."

There was a jingling noise from over the front door. Loraleigh raised her eyes expectantly. The door popped open and in walked a heavyset middle-aged man with thick black hair. He had an amiable smile and a potbelly that pushed his red flannel shirt out over the belt on his jeans.

"Hi, Bill," Loraleigh said. "What can I do for you?"

"Oh, I just need a few supplies," Bill said, with a folksy drawl. "Got any bags of fertilizer, hon?"

"In the back room," Loraleigh said. "Like always."

"Thank you, Loraleigh," Bill said with a smile. "Who are your friends? I don't think I've seen them around before."

"I'm Frank."

"And I'm his brother, Joe," Joe added.

"I'm Chet," Chet added.

"And I'm Phil," Phil said. "Glad to meet you, Mr. . . ."

"McSavage," Bill said. "Bill McSavage."

Frank's eyes widened. "McSavage? You mean you live in that mansion on top of the hill?"

"That'd be me," Bill said. "But it's not that big a deal. The house has been in my family for over a century. I work a little farm up there, and a couple of hired hands help me with it."

"Well, we're glad to meet you, Mr. McSavage," Joe said.

"If you boys have time, come on up and see me and my place," Bill said. "Always nice to have some young people visit. Now, Loraleigh, do you think you could help me fetch some fertilizer?"

"Be glad to," Loraleigh said. "Come on back here."

When Loraleigh and Bill disappeared into the back room, Joe turned to Frank and frowned. "I think we'd better get back to see how Biff's doing. I'm worried about him."

"Yeah," Frank said. "I don't care what Rhonda says. I think maybe we should think about getting outside help. Get him to a hospital. At least get his leg x-rayed so we know what the situation is."

"Do you think Rhonda has a phone?" Joe asked.

"Everybody's got a phone," Chet said.

"Not us," Frank answered, referring to the cell phone they had brought, which was dropped and broken.

"Not necessarily," Phil said. "A small percentage of the population of this country lacks phone service."

"Do they have bathrooms at least?" Joe asked.

"Not always," Phil said.

"And on that cheerful note," Frank added, "let's go back to Doc Harrison's place."

The four boys left Sugaree's Shack and strolled

back across the street to Rhonda's house. Inside, Rhonda was deep in conversation with Biff.

Biff looked up at his friends with a bright smile. He appeared not to be in any pain. "Rhonda's been telling me some interesting stuff," he said. "Man, you should hear some of her stories."

"We'd love to," Frank said, "but I'm not sure we'll have time. We talked, and we want to get you to a real hospital. I hope you're not offended, Rhonda."

Biff furrowed his brow and spoke before Rhonda could utter a word. "Hey, Rhonda's as good as any doctor at any hospital!"

"But she doesn't have the equipment to do as good a job on your leg as a real hospital would," Frank said.

"They're right, Biff," Rhonda said. "If you get in touch with the hospital in Brighton, they could probably prescribe the best course of treatment. Maybe you should go."

"Could we use your phone?" Joe asked.

"It's right over there," Rhonda said, pointing. On the nightstand next to the bed was an old-fashioned phone, one with a rotary dial instead of push buttons.

"Wow, I haven't seen one of these in years," Joe said. He dialed 0. "This will get me the operator, right?"

"It should," Rhonda said. "We're connected with the office in Brighton."

There was a ringing sound on the line, then a

36

woman answered. She asked if she could help Joe, then abruptly the line went dead.

"I was cut off," Joe said. "Is something wrong?"

"I heard something about a storm that was supposed to come through today," Rhonda said.

"A storm?" Joe asked. "We didn't see any storm."

"Well, you know, storms can be highly localized," Rhonda said. "This time of year a thunderstorm could easily occur between here and Brighton, but we couldn't see it from here or on the trail."

"Oh, terrific," Joe moaned. "We're going to have to walk all the way to Brighton."

"Don't be silly. Somebody must have a car we can borrow," Frank said, ignoring Joe's whining. "Rhonda?"

"I'm afraid mine's on the fritz," she said. "I've been waiting for a part for weeks. Bill McSavage has a truck, but I doubt he'd let you use it. Other folks have cars, but they need them."

"So walking to Brighton may be our only alternative," Joe said. "Let's grab our backpacks and go."

"Hey, are you guys deserting me?" Biff asked.

"We'll be back as soon as possible," Frank said. "Maybe with a medevac helicopter, if that's the only thing that can reach this place."

"They'll probably send an ambulance," Rhonda said. "Good luck."

"Seems like you're in good company, Biff," Frank said. "Come on, guys. Let's hit the trail."

Frank waved an arm at Joe, Chet, and Phil. They walked toward the door.

"Hope you get me a helicopter," Biff called after them.

"We'll do our best," Frank said. He opened the door, and the group walked out onto the street.

The Appalachian Trail seemed like the best and fastest route to Brighton. Frank led the way back to the place where the trail up to the main trail began.

A tall man in a jacket stood next to the path. "Where do you guys think you're going?" he asked.

"Up to the Appalachian Trail," Frank said.

"Yeah," Joe added. "We're heading to Brighton to find medical help. Our friend broke his leg."

The tall man scowled at them. "Well, you can't take the trail—the trail is closed."

"What!" Frank exclaimed. "This is an emergency!"

"Yeah," Joe said. "Our friend is injured."

"Too bad," the man said. "There's been a storm. The trail is blocked. Also, the road out of town to Brighton. There've been flash floods. Nobody can leave Morgan's Quarry until the road and path are clear."

5 Shelter from the Storm

"Oh, come on," Joe said reasonably. "We didn't see or hear any storm. And we were on the trail just a few hours ago."

"Storms come up fast," the man said. "And I don't like it when people question my authority."

"Who exactly are you?" Frank asked.

The man pulled an identification card out of his leather jacket. "I'm Paul Brickfield, sheriff of this area."

"You're in charge around here?" Joe asked.

"That's right," Brickfield said. "And I received a call an hour ago saying that all roads out of town are closed. We can't let you go back to the trail. It's too dangerous."

Phil gave Sheriff Brickfield a curious look. "We really didn't notice any storm."

"Yeah," Chet said. "The weather was perfect when we were on top of the mountain."

Sheriff Brickfield gave Chet a stern look. "So, are you meteorology students?"

"Um, no, not really," Chet said.

"I'm not a meteorology student, either," Frank said. "But this whole storm business sounds pretty bogus to me."

"Well, if you boys try to go up this path, my deputies will chase you off," Sheriff Brickfield said with a smug grin.

"Say, Sheriff, when the roads are clear how about taking our friend to Brighton? He needs to get to the hospital," Joe said.

"We'll see, when the roads are safe to travel," the sheriff answered with a slight smirk.

Joe turned to the others. "Let's go back into town. Looks like we'd better spend the night here, the way Rhonda suggested."

With a shrug of resignation, Frank led the group back into town. They stopped briefly at Rhonda's house to let Biff know he wouldn't be leaving right away. He didn't seem to mind. The group then went next door to Mrs. Hibley's house, which had brightly colored flowers in the window. Joe went to the front door and knocked.

A very elderly woman looked out, a suspicious but not unfriendly expression on her face. "Can I help you, young men?"

"Yes," Frank said. "We need a room for the night."

"Oh, you must be the hikers I heard about," she said. "Come on inside. My name is Grania Hibley."

Joe glanced at Frank. "Looks like news travels fast in this town."

"I have a wonderful room with four bunk beds," the woman said. "Would you like that?"

"I'd like any place I can lie down and rest my sore feet," Chet said.

"Then this should be perfect," Mrs. Hibley said, leading the hikers into a large room. The walls were lined with bunk beds like those in a dormitory, though it looked as if no one had stayed there in a long time.

"This house used to be popular with the young miners who worked in the quarry," Mrs. Hibley said. "Of course, that was a long time ago. I was just born then."

"This will be fine," Frank said. "Should we pay you now or before we leave?"

"Oh, don't worry about it," Mrs. Hibley said. "You boys can settle up with me tomorrow. Just come in and have supper with me in half an hour. Then you can have a nice sleep." She left the room with a smile, closing the door behind her.

41

Before the boys followed her out to the dining room, they washed up. "Looks like we're stuck in Morgan's Quarry for the night," Joe said, lathering his hands.

"And maybe longer than that," Frank added. "Sheriff Brickfield didn't look happy to let anybody go on that trail."

"If it's just a storm," Phil said, "it should clear up by tomorrow."

"Maybe," Frank said.

"Something got you suspicious?" Joe asked.

"I'm not sure," Frank said. "There's just something about this whole town."

"Yeah, I'm sensing something's wrong big time," Joe said. "But maybe we're just hungry. Let's go eat."

"I'm in favor of that," Chet said, and led the way to the dining room. It had been a long day.

The first to wake up the next morning was Chet. The aroma of pancakes and sausages filled the air.

"Smells like an old-fashioned country breakfast!" Chet declared.

Joe peered out wearily from underneath his pillow. "I feel like I've just walked a hundred and fifty miles."

"You have," Frank said. "We all have."

Chet leaped out of bed. "I don't know about you guys, but I'm ready to eat."

"Has there ever been a time when you *weren't* ready to eat?" Joe asked.

"I hope that shower has lots of hot water," Frank said. "Even after a shower last night, I've stilll got enough dirt on me to grow tomatoes."

"Tomatoes sound good," Chet declared.

After showering Chet followed his nose out into the hallway and into the dining room, just one door down from where they had been sleeping. Mrs. Hibley was busy setting plates on a large table.

"Oh, you boys are just in time," she said cheerfully. "I've made a big breakfast for you. Are you hungry?"

"You've got that right," Chet said, planting himself at the table and looking up expectantly.

"Watch out for Chet," Frank said, walking in with a groggy look on his face. "He'll eat you out of house and home."

"I don't think that's likely," Mrs. Hibley said. "I've got plenty of food."

"You haven't met Chet," Joe said, entering with Phil.

Mrs. Hibley began serving breakfast, bringing in platters filled with scrambled eggs, home fries, pancakes, and sausages. Chet piled large amounts of each item on his plate.

"Thank you very much, ma'am," Chet told Mrs. Hibley. "I think I'd like to live here."

"It's a pleasure to feed someone with such a healthy appetite," Mrs. Hibley responded.

The other teens joined Chet in digging in. Mrs. Hibley's breakfast was delicious. Joe and Frank missed their aunt Gertrude's cooking, but Mrs. Hibley's was almost as good.

Chet held out his plate. "Can I have seconds on those pancakes?"

Mrs. Hibley beamed. "Why, of course you can."

"We just love your cooking, Mrs. Hibley," Joe said. "I'd like some more of these sausages, if you don't mind."

"You're starting to sound like Chet," Frank said to his brother. "Actually, I'd like some more scrambled eggs myself."

"And home fries?" Phil asked.

"Coming right up," Mrs. Hibley said. "Oh, I just love cooking for a roomful of young men."

Joe leaned toward Frank. "So, you think we'll be able to get out of town today?"

"Hard to tell," Frank said. "We'll have to try going back to the trail again, and hope Sheriff Brickfield isn't there."

Frank finally pulled himself up from the table, his stomach full. "Great meal, Mrs. Hibley, but we have to get going."

"Oh," Mrs. Hibley said. "Won't you stay for raspberry tart?"

"I'll stay," Chet volunteered.

"No, you won't," Joe said. "But, boy, the tart sure smells good."

Frank grabbed Chet around the shoulders. "Come on, Chet. We have to go take care of Biff."

Chet struggled to break loose from Frank's grip. "Hey, I was just being polite."

"Real polite," Joe said. "If Mrs. Hibley offered you another course of sausages and home fries, you'd be here the rest of the morning."

"There's more where that came from," Mrs. Hibley said cheerfully.

"That's okay, ma'am," Frank said. We've got to be on our way."

"Hey, I was just . . ." Chet shut up abruptly when Joe tugged on his shoulder.

"Really, that was a great meal," Joe said.

"The best," Phil agreed.

Joe gave Mrs. Hibley the money for their night's stay, promising that they'd be back for their bags soon. The four teenagers walked quickly out of the dining room and through the front door. Main Street glowed brightly in the morning sunlight. Rhonda's door was unlocked, so they went in. Biff and Rhonda were engaged in a heated conversation.

"So, how's it going?" Frank asked.

"Just great," Biff said. "It was almost worth getting my leg banged up to talk to Rhonda."

"Biff's doing fine," Rhonda added. "Oh, Sheriff Brickfield stopped by and said the path and roads are still too dangerous to travel, so it looks like you'll be here a little longer."

"Oh, great," Joe moaned. "It's like everything's conspiring to keep us here."

"And that means Mrs. Hibley can keep feeding us," Chet said happily.

"At least two people are happy in this town," Frank said. "Biff and Chet."

"Well, the rest of us have to find something to keep busy," Joe said. "What do you suppose people do for fun around here?"

"Not much," Rhonda said. "Visit neighbors, watch TV."

"Hey, we could go visit that farmer guy, McSavage," Chet suggested. "He invited us to see his place."

"Doesn't sound too exciting to me," Joe said.

"You never know," Frank said. "Maybe we *should* have a look around up there."

Frank, Joe, Chet, and Phil left Rhonda's house and headed up the hill to the McSavage mansion. As they got closer, it appeared even larger than they had thought, but they could see it wasn't in very good repair. The paint was badly chipped, and a shutter was hanging partially off its hinges. The grass in the front yard burst up in patches, as though much of it had

46

been allowed to die from lack of water while the rest hadn't been cut in years.

Bill McSavage had apparently seen them coming up the hill, because he came bounding out the front door with a large grin on his face. "Hello, boys," he declared. "I've been looking forward to showing you around the place."

"Nice farm," Phil said. "What do you grow?"

"Right now," McSavage said, "mostly grasses for hay. And we've got some cows for milk. Oh, and we've got the most wonderful horse."

"Cool," Chet said. "I really like horses. Can we have a look at him?"

"Sure," McSavage said. "Formby is real friendly. He'll just love you boys."

"Would you mind if I hung around up here by the house while you guys looked at this horse?" Frank asked. "I'm, uh, something of an architecture buff, and this place seems very interesting." Joe noticed an odd look cross Frank's face, though nobody else saw it.

"Suit yourself," McSavage said. "This house dates back to the late nineteenth century and I'm sure you'll find it fascinating. The rest of you, come with me."

Joe hung back for a moment and whispered in his brother's ear. "What was that about? You're up to something."

"There's something funny about this town," Frank

47

said. "Those guys with the sack of money, that sheriff who won't let us get out of here, the storm that may have been, phones that conveniently break, and this old house watching over the whole place. I want to check it out."

"Just don't get yourself in trouble," Joe said. "Remember, Bill's got farmhands looking after this place."

Joe hurried down the hill after the others. McSavage was leading them toward an old barn. Outside the barn, in the paddock, was a large black stallion, a very impressive-looking horse.

"This is Formby," Bill said. "Any of you boys like to ride him?"

"I would," Chet said excitedly. "All I need is a saddle."

"Got one right inside," McSavage said. He walked into the barn and returned with a saddle, which he threw across Formby's back. Chet cinched it and climbed on. Formby seemed to take to Chet immediately.

"Here you go, young man," McSavage said, pulling an apple from a barrel and handing it to Chet.

Chet took the apple and leaned forward to lower it toward Formby's mouth. "You love apples, don't you, boy?" Chet asked the horse.

Abruptly Formby reared up. Something about the apple seemed to bother him. He began bucking

48

wildly, then running around in circles. It was almost as though he was trying to throw Chet off.

Caught off balance, Chet struggled to stay in the saddle. He managed to straighten up and pull hard on the reins, but that only made the stallion buck more. Somehow, Joe knew, Chet had to regain control of the horse and soon. If not, he stood a good chance of being thrown—and trampled.

6 The Horse Whisperer

"Somebody do something!" Joe cried as Chet fought desperately to stay on the horse. "Mr. McSavage, you've got to stop Formby."

McSavage held up his hands. "I don't know what's happening," he said. "I've never seen Formby like this."

As Joe and Phil watched, frantic to help their friend, Chet managed to get hold of the saddle pommel. Then he grabbed Formby's mane, one hand after the other, until he was stretched forward in the saddle, his arms wound tightly around the stallion's neck. To Joe's and Phil's astonishment, it looked as though Chet was now talking into the horse's ear.

Formby continued to buck but slowly started to calm down. Finally the wild thrashing ceased, and once again he stood calmly with Chet still on his back.

"I knew we could work things out, Formby," Chet said to the horse. "You're a good horse. I knew that all along."

"What did you do, Chet?" Phil asked.

"Yeah, I've never seen anything like that," Joe said.

"You're one lucky guy," Bill McSavage said.

"It wasn't luck," Chet said. "I've done a fair amount of riding. I've even been told I had a real talent with horses. Sometimes you just have to know how to talk to them."

"Well, you'd better get down off there," Mr. McSavage said. "Wouldn't want that to happen again."

"It won't," Chet said, staying in the saddle. "Formby and I are just getting to know each other. He's going to be fine now, aren't you, boy?"

He began to walk the horse in a circle around the barnyard. "You guys can look at the rest of the farm. Formby and I are going to spend some quality time together."

Bill McSavage slapped a hand against the side of his head. "I just figured out what happened," he said, a chagrined expression on his face. "Formby used to be a movie horse. He did stunt work and had big roles in a few westerns. His trainer taught him some tricks that he could do on cue. The apple was the signal for him to start bucking like that."

"It was . . . the apple?" Joe asked suspiciously.

"Yep," McSavage said. "I'm really sorry about that. It was all my fault. If something had happened to your friend, I could never have forgiven myself."

Joe whispered to Phil, "If the horse hates apples, how come Mr. McSavage keeps a barrel of apples in the barnyard?"

"That is really strange, all right," Phil whispered.

McSavage didn't seem to notice their conversation. He waved a hand and said, "Come on up this way. I'll show you our tractor. It's got a lot of miles on it, but it can still do the job."

"I'm sure not going to sit on the tractor," Joe whispered to Phil. "Who knows what tricks it's been trained to do?"

Only a few hundred yards away, Frank was unaware of the commotion that had just occurred down the hill. He was walking around the mansion, examining the crumbling stonework and cracked windows. It must have been quite a place in its day, but its day was long past. It would cost hundreds of thousands of dollars to fix it up, Frank estimated, and the inside was probably worse.

In fact, Frank was trying to figure a way to get a look inside the mansion. He hadn't noticed Bill locking the front door on the way out, so he walked up the wide stone steps in front and pushed on the ornate wooden door. It opened easily.

"Anybody home?" he shouted, in case some of the farmhands were around. But the mansion seemed to be deserted.

The door opened into a wide but gloomy foyer. There were heavy wooden tables on both sides, with ornately carved legs. Frank had never seen tables like these outside of an antique store or a museum. One had a dusty vase on it, with no flowers in it. The other looked as if it had probably had a vase on it at one time. Frank thought he noticed small pieces of shattered porcelain on the floor around it, probably the remains of that vase. On the left-hand wall hung a large portrait of a distinguished-looking man with muttonchop sideburns and a high, stiff white collar. At the bottom of the portrait was a name on a bronze plaque: Angus McSavage.

Probably the guy who built this place, Frank thought.

Beyond the foyer was a huge parlor, with overstuffed, maroon velvet-covered sofas all around it. Because of the amount of dust and cobwebs, Frank deduced that nobody spent much time in this room anymore.

There was a bookshelf on one wall, with quite a few books on it. Most were covered with dust, but one appeared to be quite clean and looked as if somebody might actually read it from time to time. It was titled *The Roaring Twenties: End of an Era.* When Frank pulled it down and glanced through it, the book fell open to one particularly well-thumbed page. On it was a picture of the mansion he was now standing inside. The photo had been taken in 1928, and the house had clearly been in better shape than it was now. Women in knee-length flapper dresses with long ropes of pearls and men in well-tailored suits and bowler hats were standing in the front yard and on the steps. A man who looked like the portrait of Angus McSavage was in the middle of the crowd. He was probably about seventy years old.

On the opposite page the house was mentioned by name as the McSavage Mansion. Frank began reading.

According to the book, Angus McSavage had bought the granite quarry for which the town was named sometime in the late nineteenth century, from a man named Joshua Morgan. Frank remembered that this was what Loraleigh had told them, which meant her family had been here even longer than the McSavages. The quarry made the McSavages wealthy and allowed them to build this mansion, but the granite ran out in the 1920s. By then, however, Angus McSavage had gotten into another line of business. After Prohibition became law in 1920, he turned the mansion into a speakeasy. It had been quite notorious during the 1920s and early 1930s. It had also been an inn, so rich people would come to spend their weekends there—and sometimes the whole week. Angus McSavage had some political influence, and the police never shut his operation down. But the end of Prohibition in 1933 had ruined his business. Nobody went to speakeasies anymore. The book didn't mention what had happened to the mansion after that.

Frank looked around again at the ancient furniture and unvacuumed carpet. The place was a mess, but it looked as if it had been taken care of more recently than 1933. Maybe the McSavage granite quarry had still brought in a little money, though nothing in the book indicated that to be so. Or maybe the McSavage farm had provided enough income, though from what Frank had seen it didn't look like much of a farm. But obviously the family had continued making money—and at some point, judging from the poor condition of the house, the flow of money had stopped. Since the mansion was probably the economic center of the entire town, the local prosperity must have dried up at the same time.

A room off to one side of the parlor caught Frank's eye. It appeared to be an office of some kind. In it was a large desk and rows of ledgers on shelves. This must be where the McSavage family took care of the quarry and the speakeasy business, Frank reasoned. He opened one of the ledgers. Inside was a list of names with a dollar amount next to each one; some had plus signs next to them and some minus signs. The names were those of individuals and the dates next to the transactions were relatively recent, from the 1960s and 1970s.

"Can I help you?" said an extremely deep voice from behind Frank.

Frank dropped the book, startled. He turned to see a tall man about sixty years old. He was stiff and imperious looking, like a butler in an old movie. He looked as if he should be wearing a tuxedo instead of the jeans and flannel shirt he did wear. Frank guessed that he probably was a McSavage household employee, though how Bill could afford household help when he couldn't afford to keep up the house, Frank couldn't imagine.

"I was, um, lost," Frank said, fumbling for an explanation as to why he was prying through the books. "Mr. McSavage said I could look around the house while he and my friends toured the farm. I was trying to find the way out."

"Are you sure," the butler asked, "that Mr. McSavage gave you permission to look around the *inside* of the house? Perhaps he was referring to the grounds."

"Oh," Frank said, trying to look convincingly puzzled. "I'm not sure. Maybe I misunderstood him. Well, if you'll show me where the exit is . . ."

"Right through there," the man said, pointing to a

door Frank hadn't noticed before. "Why don't you step on through?"

Frank hesitated. He wasn't really lost and knew that the door couldn't possibly lead to the front entrance. But maybe the man wanted him to go out through some kind of side entrance. Frank pulled the door open and walked through.

There was a grinding noise behind him, as though the man were operating some kind of machine. Frank started to turn, but instantly began to lose his balance.

The floor slid open beneath him. All at once Frank was falling through the blackness of empty space!

7 All Bets Are Off

Frank landed on a hard surface. The force of the fall left him stunned for a moment. He had fallen through a trapdoor, he realized. And the trapdoor that he had fallen through, which was about eight feet above where he was now standing, slid neatly closed. All at once Frank was in total darkness.

He shook his head, trying to get his senses back. Obviously, the man didn't want Frank to leave the house. But why? What had Frank seen that he wasn't supposed to see? The stuff about the house having been a speakeasy during Prohibition? That was apparently well known, since it had been written up in a history book. The old ledgers? Frank had no idea what the ledgers meant.

Whatever the problem, it was clear that the first

order of business was to find his way out of here. Frank reached in his pocket and pulled out a small box of kitchen matches that he had used for lighting campfires on the trail. He lit a match and looked around. He seemed to be in a very large room, and the faint light from the match didn't reach all the way to the walls. He could make out strange dark objects, some about the size and shape of a small man, some more like large tables. All were covered with drop cloths.

The match guttered out, but not before Frank spotted an oil lamp on top of one of the drop cloths. He groped for it in the dark and sniffed at it. It smelled as if it still had some oil in it. He fumbled with a second match and managed to light the lamp.

He could see better now, but he still had no idea what the strange dark objects were. He lifted the drop cloth off one. Underneath was a slot machine. Was this something the McSavage family kept around the house for fun? Frank walked to one of the large covered objects and removed the cloth. Underneath was a roulette table. He pulled off several more cloths and found a blackjack table and two more slot machines. There were more large cloth-covered objects as far as he could see in the darkness. No way was this the McSavage family recreation room.

It all made sense, Frank thought. This place was a casino. That must be how the McSavage family made their money after Prohibition ended. In fact, old Angus McSavage had probably opened the casino as part of the speakeasy. The mansion had been filled with wealthy vacationers, and this was another way to separate them from their money. When the speakeasy closed, the casino must have become the family's main source of income. The granite quarry had played out years before, and the farm was probably never more than a front.

But why had the casino folded? Frank thought about it for a moment. If he remembered his history correctly, casinos were illegal in most of the United States back in the 1920s and for many years afterward. An illegal casino as nice as this one probably didn't have much competition in this area. Angus McSavage had the gambling market pretty much locked up.

In 1978 New Jersey had made casino gambling legal in Atlantic City, and that had probably drawn off most of the McSavage family's customers. Anyone would have preferred going to a legal casino in New Jersey over an illegal one in the middle of the woods. The New Jersey casinos were probably easier to reach, as well. There weren't any superhighways or airports to Morgan's Quarry.

The loss of the casino had probably hurt the town as well. A lot of the citizens of Morgan's Quarry probably worked in the casino and got a piece of the money that the McSavage family was bringing in. When the casino died, so did the town's economy.

That still didn't explain why nobody wanted the boys to leave town. The casino was obviously a thing of the past. There didn't seem to be anything illegal going on here now.

Or was there?

Frank thought about the two men he and his friends had seen on the way into town carrying the large bag filled with money. The money couldn't have come from the casino, which had obviously been closed for a long time. So where *had* it come from?

He could worry about that later. Before the lamp burned out, Frank had to find a way out of the basement—or he was going to be in a lot of trouble, just as Loraleigh had predicted.

Meanwhile, Joe was starting to get worried about his brother. He and Phil had gotten back into town after their tour of the McSavage farm. It had been pretty boring because it wasn't much of a farm. Joe wondered how anybody could make a living from it. Only Chet had enjoyed their little excursion. He was still off riding the horse. Phil went to Mrs. Hibley's to talk to the old woman about the history of Morgan's Quarry.

Joe had expected to find Frank back at the mansion, but there was no sign of him. So he returned to Rhonda's house, thinking Frank might have gone there. But neither Rhonda nor Biff had seen Frank. He stopped for a quick lunch at Mrs. Hibley's. Phil had left, Mrs. Hibley said, to explore the old quarry site. He thought maybe he could find some fossilized trilobites. Frank wasn't there, either.

That meant Frank must still be back at the mansion, and that meant something might have gone wrong.

Joe decided to pay another visit to Sugaree's Shack. Maybe Loraleigh could give him some advice about locating his brother. She seemed like a pretty decent person, despite the cryptic remark she had made the day before about all of them winding up in trouble.

When Joe walked into the general store, Loraleigh had some customers, two wiry tough-looking men in their twenties, dressed in ragged jeans and T-shirts. They looked suspiciously familiar. Wait a minute, Joe thought. These are the two guys who were carrying that sack of money yesterday!

"Who are you lookin' at?" one of the men asked sourly.

"Sorry," Joe said. "I don't mean to cause trouble."

Loraleigh looked worried. "Joe, these are the Brookburn brothers. They work as farmhands up at Bill McSavage's place."

"Glad to meet you," Joe said, extending a hand.

The brothers ignored Joe's hand. "Well, we ain't so glad to see you," one of them said. "We don't like strangers in this town."

"Yeah, nobody invited you here," the other one said.

Joe started getting angry. "And we don't want to be here. This town is a lousy place to get stuck in."

"This is our town," the first brother growled. "Those are fighting words."

"Yeah," the second brother said. "Step outside. We'll work this out."

Joe began to get worried. He was a pretty good fighter, but these guys had serious muscles—and they had him outnumbered. The last thing he wanted was to get caught in a fight with them.

"No, thanks," Joe said. "I think I'll stay in here."

"What are you, some sort of a little coward?" the first brother said.

"Yeah, I think you're a coward," the second brother said. "And I don't like cowards."

"You watch who you call a coward!" Joe snapped, his anger getting the better of him. "And I don't like guys who pick fights with strangers!"

"Then let's go outside," the first brother said, advancing on Joe.

Joe began to get a little nervous. Maybe he should make a break for the door now—but the brothers were too close. They might beat him to the door—and then where could he go?

"Get moving!" the second brother said. Something flashed in his right hand.

Joe glanced down and saw that the man was holding a very long and very sharp-looking knife.

8 To the Rescue!

"No!" Loraleigh cried. "Please don't do that!"

"Mind your own business, young lady," the first brother said. "We've got to teach this young man a lesson."

"Now step outside like we asked," the second brother told Joe. "And then we'll find out if you really are a coward."

Joe backed toward the door, still looking for a way out. "This isn't a fair fight."

"Aw, now, ain't that too bad," the first brother said.

Joe pushed the door open and stepped out into the street. He was thinking of making a run for it, but one of the brothers stepped quickly to the other side of him so that he was surrounded.

"Which of us should fight him first?" the second brother asked.

"Maybe we should fight him together," the first brother said.

The second brother smiled. "I like that idea."

They moved in on Joe. With the first brother holding a knife on him, Joe looked around desperately for an escape route.

Suddenly hoofbeats thundered from behind Joe. Chet! Joe crouched and planted himself as Chet slowed Formby. As Chet rode by, Joe placed his hands on Formby's rump and vaulted onto his back, throwing his arms around Chet for balance. The Brookburn brothers ran after them for a moment but quickly gave up the chase.

Chet rounded a corner, where they were out of sight of the Brookburn brothers.

"Thanks, pal," Joe said. "You might have saved my life back there."

"You looked like you needed rescuing," Chet said. "Those guys look mean."

"As mean as rattlesnakes," Joe said. "Even meaner. After all, rattlesnakes are just acting in self-defense."

"So where's Frank?" Chet asked. "He's usually your backup."

"I don't know," Joe said. "Frank was snooping around that old mansion earlier, but now I can't find him anywhere."

"Maybe you should check out the mansion," Chet suggested.

"My idea exactly," Joe said. "But I'd like to know something about the place first. I was hoping Loraleigh could tell me something."

"Well, here's your chance to ask her about it," Chet said.

Loraleigh was just stepping out the back door of Sugaree's Shack. She looked up at Joe in astonishment.

"Oh, thank goodness," she said. "You're okay. I was just going to get some help."

"Thanks," Joe said, dismounting. "Do those guys always play so rough?"

"The Brookburn brothers are tough men," Loraleigh said. "They have to be. They're the only farmhands that Bill has, and they do a lot of hard manual work."

"Does that work include pulling knives on innocent people?" Joe asked.

"No," she said. "I've never seen them do anything like that. Get into a few brawls with their fists, maybe, but I've never seen them pull a knife."

"Well, it looks like those 'tough' guys are moving up into the big leagues," Joe said. "Probably get themselves thrown into jail real soon." He changed the subject. "Listen, I think something's happened to Frank. The last time I saw him was up at the McSavage mansion."

Loraleigh's face darkened. "That's not good," she

66

said. "He—" She stopped herself, as though re-membering there was something important she shouldn't say.

"He what?" Joe asked. "Listen, Loraleigh, if there's anything you know that will help Frank, you'd better tell me now."

"There's a storm cellar entrance on the east side of the mansion. Here's the key." She pulled a small key out of her jeans pocket and dropped it in Joe's hand.

"Where'd you get this?" Joe asked.

"I sometimes deliver stuff right to Bill's house," Loraleigh said. "Don't let him know where you got this key."

"Believe me," Joe said, "I won't. Thanks a lot, Lo-raleigh."

"Need a lift up to the mansion?" Chet asked.

"You bet," Joe said. "It's a long walk up the hill."

The two took off up the road that led to Bill McSav-age's mansion. Chet dropped Joe in the nearby woods, where they weren't visible from the front windows.

"Want me to come with you?" Chet asked.

"No, thanks," Joe said. "I'm going to do some sneaking around. It'd be better if I did it by myself. Less conspicuous."

"I'll take Formby back to the barn," Chet said. "Come on, boy!"

Chet rode away as Joe walked through the woods. Bill McSavage's mansion was about a hundred feet away. Joe made his way through the trees, sneaking up on the mansion.

Sure enough, there was the door to the storm cellar, just where Loraleigh had said it would be. It was an old-fashioned cellar door made of wood, set into the ground with a small mound of weathered bricks around it. Apparently it led down into the basement. There was a rusty old latch in the middle of the door with a fairly new looking padlock holding it shut.

Joe looked up at the windows to see if anybody was watching. Then he darted across to the cellar door and slipped the key into the padlock.

The padlock was stiff, and for a moment Joe thought it might not open. He tugged on it until it finally gave.

The hinges were rusted so tight that Joe had to pull with all of his strength to get it to open even after unlocking it. Finally the door came open, a cloud of dust flying up. All he could see below was a pitch-black hole, barely penetrated by the sunlight.

Joe extended his foot gingerly inside and found the stone tread of a carved stone staircase. He turned around so he could back down the steep stairs, using his hands to balance himself. Slowly he began to descend, worried that he'd miss his footing.

The stairs went down about seven feet before Joe felt his foot touch the floor. The room was dark, with no sign of a light switch or light bulb. The sunlight from above was of little help. The room he was in was so dark that the tiny sliver of sun couldn't begin to illuminate it.

He stretched out a hand and felt a stone wall. Okay, so this was the basement of the mansion, he thought. What could be down here?

Suddenly a hand gripped his shoulder and a gruff voice said, "Make another move, mister, and you've had it!"

9 Hay Ride

Joe spun around. To his relief, he saw that it was his brother, Frank, standing behind him. He had come to find Frank and rescue him, but Frank had found him instead.

"Boy, you scared me!" Frank cried.

"*I* scared *you?*" Joe gasped. "How would you like to have somebody sneak up behind you like that?"

"Been there, done that," Frank said.

"So how did you end up down here?" Joe asked. "I've been looking all over for you."

"I've got a quite a lot to tell you," Frank said.

"You'd better," Joe said. "I think you were right when you said that there were some strange things going on in this town."

"Yep," Frank said. "And I know what some of

those things are." Frank relit the oil lamp, which he was still holding. "I want to take you on a quick tour of this place."

"What kind of tour?" Joe asked. "Is this a museum or something?"

"Sort of," Frank said. "A museum of criminal activities from the past."

"Wow," Joe said. "Sounds like my kind of museum."

Frank led Joe to where he had uncovered the slot machines and gaming tables. "Get a load of this stuff."

Joe's eyes widened. "This looks like something out of Las Vegas. But what's it all doing here? Casinos are illegal in this area. And, as far as I know, they always have been."

Frank told Joe what he had learned from the book upstairs and what he had figured out on his own.

"Ha!" Joe laughed. "I never believed that Bill McSavage was a farmer. And he practically killed Chet with that horse—deliberately, I'm pretty sure."

"I think there are people in this town that want all of us dead," Frank said.

Joe looked stunned. "But why?"

"I think there's some kind of illegal operation still going on around here. And they think we know something about it," Frank explained.

"But what do we know about . . ." Joe's eyes began to gleam. "That money we saw those guys drop yesterday!"

"Exactly," Frank said. "We weren't supposed to see that. And that's why they don't want us leaving town. We might tell somebody about it, somebody who'll figure out where that money came from."

"But who is 'they'?" Joe asked. "Who wants us dead?"

"Well, I'm guessing that Bill McSavage does, for starters," Frank said.

"Yeah," Joe said. "And the Brookburn brothers, too."

"Who are the Brookburn brothers?" Frank asked.

"The guys who were carrying the money," Joe said. "I had a kind of nasty encounter with them a few minutes ago. They seem to be Bill's farmhands—and maybe his partners in crime, too."

"I think Bill's manservant is part of it," Frank said. "Wait till you get a load of that guy."

"Manservant?" Joe asked. "I thought manservants just existed in old novels."

There was a creaking noise from above. Somebody had slid open the trapdoor that Frank had fallen through, and light was filtering down into the cellar. A pair of arms shoved a ladder through the hole.

"They exist for real," Frank said. "And here's the gentleman now."

"We'd better move," Joe whispered. "Fast."

"Who are you talking to?" the butler bellowed from above. "Mr. McSavage wants to see you right now, young man, and if you've got somebody down there with you, you'd better get him here right now, too, if he knows what's good for him!"

Frank and Joe took off for the cellar stairs that led outside. Joe raced up first. As Frank climbed up after him, he looked back to see the butler leap off the bottom rung of the ladder—with a rifle slung over his shoulders.

"Get a move on!" Frank urged. "We're being followed by a crazy guy with a gun!"

Joe climbed out onto the ground, and said, "Now what have you gotten us into? Here I was just trying to save your life!"

"You may have helped," Frank said. "Now we've got to get away from here. But which way should we go?"

"Not back toward town," Joe said, padlocking the cellar door closed. Seconds later there was a pounding from below, as the man tried to get out.

"We can make a run for the barn," Frank said.

"Better than nothing," Joe said. "Maybe we can hitch a ride on Chet's horse."

The brothers began running down the hill toward the barn. They could hear frantic noises from the mansion behind them. Just as they were about to pass beyond sight of the old house the front door opened and the servant and Bill McSavage came bursting out. They were both carrying rifles.

The barn door was partially opened, and the brothers slipped inside and looked around. The horse was nowhere to be seen, but there were two large piles of hay on the floor, one of them as large as a shed.

"Bill doesn't have much of a farm, but he sure makes a lot of hay," Joe said. "I wonder why he keeps such a big pile of it."

"Just get inside it," Frank said.

Joe gave the haystack a dirty look. "Looks worse than the campsites we slept in on the trail."

"It beats getting shot," Frank said, shoving his brother into the haystack. They both burrowed into the stiff bristles of dried grass, trying to disappear while still being able to breathe.

From the direction of the barn door, they could hear the sound of voices. "I think they're in here," said the voice of the servant. "I thought I saw them heading in this direction."

"I'm not so sure, Quentin," Bill McSavage said. "I think they may have gone back into the fields. I'm heading up there. You take a look around here. That pitchfork might help. If you don't find them, join me."

"And if I do find them?"

"You know what to do." Bill McSavage's footsteps disappeared quickly into the distance.

The door creaked open. The servant, Quentin, could be heard walking across the dried hay that littered the floor of the barn.

Frank shuddered as he remembered what Bill had

just said about a pitchfork. Quentin must be about to poke the fork into the haystacks to see if we're hiding in them. A quick poke with a pitchfork could hurt a lot—or it could be fatal!

There was the sound of metal scraping against the floor as Quentin picked up the pitchfork, then the sound of the pitchfork being pushed into dry grass. Quentin was poking at a haystack, but it wasn't the one that Frank and Joe were hiding in. Frank almost sighed with relief, but he didn't want Quentin to hear him. And it was unlikely that the man would give up after a single poke.

The sound of the pitchfork came again, this time closer to where Frank was hiding. He kept as still as he could. Then the pitchfork stabbed straight into the large haystack, right between Frank's legs! Frank willed himself to stay still. He didn't want to give himself and Joe away. The pitchfork lashed into the hay again, this time inches from Frank's bicep. If Quentin aimed just a few inches to the right, Frank was a goner!

But the next stab into the hay sounded slightly farther away, though Quentin was still examining the haystack the Hardys had plunged into. Frank started to relax as Quentin moved away, but then he started worrying about Joe. What if Quentin had stabbed his brother?

There was another sharp thrust from the pitchfork,

but it didn't seem to touch anything except hay. Another thrust followed, and Frank heard an odd noise, as if the pitchfork had struck metal.

Metal? Maybe, thought Frank, Quentin had found a needle in a haystack.

The sound of the metal seemed to distract Quentin. He wandered away and could be heard putting the pitchfork back against the wall. Stable doors creaked as Quentin checked the horse stalls, then the outer door opened. Frank could hear Quentin leave.

Just to be sure, though, he stood quietly in the hay for another minute. Finally he peeked out. There was no sign of Quentin.

"I think it's safe to come out," Frank whispered. "Are you okay, Joe?"

"Yeah," his brother said. "But that pitchfork scared me almost as much as the gun did."

Frank crawled out of the hay. Unless Quentin was crouching in a horse stall, the man was gone.

There was a rustling noise as Joe began to climb out from beneath the hay. Then there was a clanking sound.

"Ouch!" Joe exclaimed loudly from beneath the hay. Then his face appeared, contorted with pain.

"Keep your voice down!" Frank whispered. "Do you want those guys to hear us?"

76

"I just banged my head on something really hard," Joe said, trying to keep his voice down. "Wow, does it hurt!"

"Maybe what you hit was the same thing I heard Quentin hit with the pitchfork," Frank said. "Was it metal?"

"I don't know," Joe said. "I was too busy feeling pain to do a chemical analysis on it."

Frank helped Joe stand up. Then he began digging in the huge stack of hay.

"What are you looking for?" Joe asked. "A needle in a—"

"I already thought of that joke," Frank said. "There's something under this hay."

"What's the big deal?" Joe said. "Probably just an old plow somebody left lying here in 1888." But he started digging, too.

Something very large was under the hay, but it wasn't a plow. As the brothers began to uncover it, they could see that it was indeed metal and was freshly painted.

"That's not from 1888," Joe said, a baffled expression on his face. "It looks brand-new. A lot newer than anything else in this town."

"Yeah," Frank said. "It's a truck. But why would they keep a truck in a haystack?"

"Maybe they couldn't afford a garage," Joe said, and laughed at his joke.

As they brushed the hay off the truck, Frank stood back to get a good look at it.

"I think maybe we've found the answer to our mystery," he said.

Joe nodded. "Yeah, now I think I know what Bill McSavage and his friends have been hiding."

The truck was small with a cab designed for two people and a squared-off rear end. On the side it read Pinkerby's Armored Transport.

"Looks like the kind of truck banks use to move money," Joe said.

"Let's see what's inside," Frank suggested.

He walked to the back door. It wasn't locked. He opened the bolt and pulled the door open. Even in the dim light of the barn they could see what the truck contained. Dozens of large sacks, like the one they had seen the Brookburn brothers carrying the day before, were piled up inside. The sacks were stuffed full of something and it was pretty obvious what that something was because it was spilling out of several bags—$100 bills, bound together with paper seals, like those in a bank vault.

"This thing is full of money!" Joe exclaimed.

"It sure is," Frank said. "There must be millions of dollars in here!"

10 The Lady Vanishes

"Where did all this come from?" Joe wondered. "Millions of dollars don't just pop out of thin air."

"Especially with a truck conveniently wrapped around them," Frank said. "Hey, you remember that robbery a few months ago down in Cold Ridge?"

"Oh, right," Joe said. "Somebody got away with a truckload of cash. The cops never caught them."

"Well, I think we're looking at that truckload right now," Frank said.

"But Cold Ridge is hundreds of miles from here," Joe said.

"True," Frank said. "But whoever stole this would have wanted to move it far from the scene of the crime. They'd want to hide it someplace nobody would think to look."

"And nobody *would* have looked if we hadn't stumbled into this little town," Joe said. "I don't think they were expecting visitors."

"And they didn't like visitors when they got them," Frank said. "That's why we've felt so unwelcome here."

"We have to tell somebody about this," Joe said.

"Yeah, but who?" Frank asked. "I bet Sheriff Brickfield is in on this, too."

"We can go to Loraleigh," Joe said. "She seems to be okay."

"I think you're right about Loraleigh," Frank said. "But how could she help us? We might just be putting her in danger."

Joe shivered. "It looks like *all* of our lives are in danger. Me, you, Chet, Phil—and Biff."

"Biff should be okay with Rhonda," Frank said.

"True," Joe said. "She looks pretty tough. But if McSavage and his hired hands come to her place to get Biff, she'll be outnumbered."

"We'd better get out of this barn and off this farm," Frank said. "Bill and Quentin are probably still looking for us in the fields, but they might not be quite so brazen about trying to kill us if we were back in town."

"We can only hope," Joe said.

The brothers walked to the door of the barn and peered out. Neither Quentin nor Bill was in sight. The brothers slipped through the wooden doors and headed for the fence that surrounded the farm. It wasn't hard to get over the fence, but on the other side was thick underbrush. It took them fifteen minutes to fight their way through it and get back to town.

As they skulked onto Main Street, hoping that nobody from McSavage's farm would notice them, they were surprised to see Phil Cohen running toward them, a frightened look on his face.

"Come quick!" he cried. "You've got to see what happened!"

"Wait till we tell *you* what happened," Joe said, but it was clear that Phil was very upset over something. He and Frank followed Phil to Rhonda's house.

The front door was wide open. Mrs. Hibley was standing outside, looking as if she was about to faint.

"Maybe Biff will tell us what happened," Frank said, stepping inside. "Hey, Biff! Where are you?"

"That's the problem," Phil said. "He isn't here. Not in the house, anyway."

"What?" Joe said. "Then where's Rhonda."

"She's not here, either," Phil said. "According to Mrs. Hibley, who saw part of it, these two big guys— I think they were the ones we saw carrying that money yesterday—came here and left with Rhonda and Biff. At gunpoint!"

"It was terrible!" Mrs. Hibley cried, standing in the doorway. "I've never seen anything like it!"

"The Brookburn brothers," Frank said. "They've kidnapped Rhonda and Biff!"

"How did they get Biff out of here?" Joe asked. "He couldn't walk."

"He was on crutches," Mrs. Hibley said.

"Do you know where they took them?" Frank asked.

"Oh, no," Mrs. Hibley said. "I didn't see where they went. I had to go sit down." She still looked as though she was going to faint.

"There's only one thing to do," Frank said.

"Yeah," Joe said. "Ask Loraleigh. I think she knows some things she hasn't told us."

Frank, Joe, and Phil crossed the street to Loraleigh's store, but the door was locked. Frank knocked five times, then peered in the window.

"She must have gone home," he said. "She said she lived right up the block, didn't she?"

"Yeah," Joe said. "I think that's her house there."

They walked a couple of houses up the street to an old house with a dilapidated front porch. The name Mason was on the mailbox. Frank knocked on the door.

After a moment Loraleigh opened the door. She was obviously scared of something.

"I don't want to speak to you," she said, starting to close the door in their faces.

"You'd better speak with us," Frank said. "Bill Mc-

Savage and his farmhands just tried to kill us. And they've kidnapped Biff and Rhonda."

Loraleigh closed her eyes in anguish. "Oh, no! I wanted to protect all of you from this."

"Well, it's too late now," Joe said. "We're in this up to our eyeballs."

"Who's that, Loraleigh?" asked a man's voice from the living room.

A middle-aged man with a muscular physique and gray hair appeared behind Loraleigh.

"It's nothing, Dad," Loraleigh said. "You can go back and watch TV."

"Actually, Mr. Mason," Frank said, "we'd like to talk with you, too."

Loraleigh's father eyed them suspiciously. "Who are you young men, anyway?"

"We're hikers, Mr. Mason," Joe explained, telling him about Biff's accident and how he had been staying at Rhonda's house.

"Rhonda Harrison's a good person," Mr. Mason said. "If she's taken you boys in, you're okay with me."

"Unfortunately, something seems to have happened to Rhonda," Frank said.

"And Biff, too," Joe added. "They've been kidnapped."

"Kidnapped?" Mr. Mason exclaimed, sharp concern showing on his face. "How did this happen?"

83

"We believe it was the Brookburn brothers from the McSavage farm," Frank said.

"I've never liked those fellows," Mr. Mason said. "They're not good people. They're too much like the people who worked at the McSavage farm in the . . . old days."

"You mean when the casino was running?" Frank asked.

Mr. Mason's face turned white. "How do you know about the casino?"

"We've seen it," Joe said. "Big as life and twice as full of cobwebs."

"I used to work there when I was young," Mr. Mason said. "I was a blackjack dealer. Bill was a pit boss, working for his father. But I felt dirty, working for an illegal business, so I left."

"Well," Joe said, "it looks like Bill's behind the kidnapping."

Mr. Mason looked startled. "Bill? He's not a very ethical man, but I've never known him to be involved in anything like kidnapping."

"Maybe murder, too," Frank said, "if we're not careful."

"No," Mr. Mason said. "All of this is impossible!"

"I'm afraid some things have changed, Dad," Loraleigh said. "I've heard things at the shop."

"Things?" Mr. Mason said. "What kind of things?"

"Bank robbery, for one, Mr. Mason," Joe said.

"It's true, Dad," Loraleigh said. "I've been pretty sure of it for at least a month. Bill and those Brookburn boys stole an armored truck full of cash down in Cold Ridge five months ago. I heard one of the brothers knew a guard at a bank who helped him on the inside. They've been keeping the truck hidden up in McSavage's barn."

"Why didn't you tell me about this?" Mr. Mason said.

"I didn't want to get you in trouble with Bill," Loraleigh said. "I know he's an old friend of yours—well, he was a friend of yours years ago—but he's a dangerous man. There's no telling what he might do."

"We have a pretty good idea," Joe said. "He and that servant of his came after us with rifles and pitchforks less than an hour ago, and I don't think they were inviting us to go hunting."

Mr. Mason slapped a fist angrily into his palm. "It's my fault. I should have done something about Bill McSavage years ago, when he was running that casino."

"It wouldn't have done you any good," Loraleigh said. "The authorities knew all about the casino, but Bill had some sort of arrangement with them."

"Arrangement spelled M-O-N-E-Y," Joe said.

"I want to see Bill McSavage," Mr. Mason said. "He's got a lot to answer for!"

"Well, we'd like to see him, too," Frank said. "He's got Rhonda and our friend Biff."

As if in answer to their wishes, three familiar faces appeared behind them in the door: Quentin's and those of the two Brookburn brothers.

"Mr. McSavage would like to see you two," Quentin said. "Up at his mansion." He cocked the barrel of the rifle for dramatic effect. "And he wants to see you *right now!*"

11 All Wired Up

"So it's *you*, Quentin," Mr. Mason snarled.

"You've never much liked me," Quentin said. "Well, the feeling is mutual. I've never much liked you, either."

"You're nothing but a common criminal, Quentin," Mr. Mason said. "Bill pulled you out of the gutter and put you in charge of all his gambling operations."

"I'd love to stick around and chat," Quentin said, "but I'm afraid the Brookburn brothers and I have been asked to accompany you up to the mansion. So, come along. All of you!"

At Quentin's urging, Frank, Joe, Phil, Loraleigh, and Mr. Mason stepped out the front door and into the street. The Brookburn brothers gave Joe a particularly nasty look as he walked past them.

Frank and Joe headed up the procession, as they walked toward the house on top of the hill. Quentin walked beside the Hardys, just far enough away so they couldn't grab the rifle from his hand. The Brookburn brothers brought up the rear, guns at the ready.

The door to the mansion was closed. Frank opened it and walked into the foyer. Quentin stepped forward and led them through the large main room and into a small study. Bill McSavage was sitting in a large overstuffed chair at the far end of the room.

"What's this about you stealing an armored truck?" Mr. Mason snapped when he saw his old friend.

"Quiet, Jack," McSavage said. "You and me don't have anything to talk about anymore."

"It sounds like we do," Mr. Mason said. "I should have turned you in to the law a long time ago. It was only a matter of time before you'd do something as stupid as pull off a robbery. And I hear you're guilty of kidnapping now, too!"

McSavage sneered. "That's true. I've just kidnapped *you*, after all."

"Why did you bring us up here?" Joe asked.

"You know too much," McSavage said. "It's dangerous to let you run around loose. I'm going to have to keep you locked up here at the house for a while until I decide what to do with you."

"I don't suppose you'll decide to let us go," Frank said.

"That doesn't seem likely," McSavage said. "Jack Mason here will blab everything—and I suspect the rest of you will start talking as soon as you're out of this town. No, I can't let you go."

Loraleigh looked startled. "Then . . . that means . . ."

"He won't get away with kidnapping us," Frank said. "I won't let him."

"My, you're a brave young man," McSavage said with a laugh. "Quentin, why don't you show these folks to the room where they'll be spending the night?"

"I'd be glad to, sir," the man said, looking at Frank, Joe, and friends with contempt.

Jack Mason put an arm around his daughter's shoulders. "I'll protect you, honey. You know I wouldn't let anything happen to you."

Quentin led them back out of the study, the Brookburn brothers once again bringing up the rear. The servant led them to an ornate staircase that took them up to the second floor. Down the long hall were several rooms. Quentin ushered the group into one.

Two people were already there: Biff and Rhonda. They looked up when the others entered. For a moment they seemed pleased to see the others, until they realized that their friends were captives, too.

"Hey!" Biff cried. "It's good to see you guys! I mean, it's nice to . . . er, I was hoping to . . ."

"See us somewhere outside this house?" Joe said. "Yeah, we were trying to rescue you, but it looks like we've wound up getting locked up with you."

Quentin left the room, closing the door behind him. There was the sound of a latch being fastened.

The room was oddly furnished with a long table with several chairs along one side of it. On the table were half a dozen or so old telephones that looked as though they hadn't been used in a while. Frank picked up a phone receiver and put it to his ear. There was no dial tone.

"It's dead," he said. "Too bad."

"What is this place, anyway?" Joe said. "Why all these telephones?"

"Yeah, Rhonda and I have been wondering about that, too," Biff said.

"I think I know," Frank said. "This place used to be a casino, right?"

"News to me," Biff said.

"Yeah, we discovered the old equipment in the basement," Joe said. "They've got roulette tables, slot machines, the works."

"And this room must have been for placing bets," Frank said. "Not on the gambling in the basement, but on other things, like horse races and sporting events."

"You mean, the McSavages were bookies, too?" Joe asked.

"Sure," Frank said. "It looks like McSavage's family

had an off-track betting operation a long time before it was legal."

"This doesn't do us any good if we can't call out," Biff said, frowning. "I'm sorry, guys. I really got us into a mess."

"It's not your fault, Biff," Frank said.

"Oh, I'm not so sure about that," Joe said jokingly. "If Biff hadn't hurt his leg—"

"Ahem!" Phil Cohen cleared his throat loudly. "Maybe these phones can do us some good after all."

"Huh?" Joe said. "Only if we hit Quentin over the head with a couple of them."

"No, that's not what I mean," Phil said. "Look at those wires."

Everybody followed Phil's gaze. All of the phone wires ran through a single round hole in the wall.

"What about them?" Joe asked.

"They have to go somewhere, right?" Phil said.

"Yeah?" Joe shrugged. "So how does that help us?"

"Look closely at the wall," Phil said.

Frank looked. He noticed what appeared to be the outline of a door that had been plastered over. It was directly over the hole where the wires disappeared. "What do you know," Frank said. "There used to be a closet here."

"Not a closet," Phil said. "A telephone exchange. The phones in this room are old, and it must have required some major equipment to keep all of them

91

working, especially when the betting got heavy. They didn't have miniaturized electronics when this place was in its heyday."

"So what good does that do us?" Joe asked.

"I'm not sure," Phil said, "but I'd like to take a look at the equipment. Just because these phones are dead doesn't mean the equipment doesn't work. If we can get through that wall, maybe we can manage to make a call out of here."

"It's worth a shot," Frank said. "Anybody got something I can use to break a hole in that wall?"

"Try this," Biff said, holding up a metal crutch. "But don't break it. I'll need it if we get out of here."

Frank took the crutch and bashed softly at the wall, trying not to make so much noise that Quentin would come running. Paint began chipping off the wall. Finally a hole began to appear in the wallboard about halfway up the wall.

Frank thrust his fingers through the hole and pulled out chunks of wallboard. The others joined in, and soon they had a hole large enough to walk through.

The room on the other side of the wall was about the size of a walk-in closet. It had no electric lights, but enough light spilled in from the main room to make the interior of the room visible. Wires were scattered all around, coiled on the floor like snakes and tangled like spiderwebs along the walls.

"Okay, let me take a look," Phil said.

"Better you than me," Joe said. "A person could get electrocuted in there!"

Phil stepped cautiously into the room, careful not to trip over the piles of wires. He looked around, studying the dimly lit walls. A look of recognition came over his face.

"This is an entire telephone switching station," he said delightedly. "It probably dates back to the 1940s. Every telephone wire in the town must run through this room!"

"Terrific!" Biff said. "Grab a phone, plug it in, and make a call to somebody who can get us out of here."

"It's not that easy," Phil said. "I'm not sure what all these wires do. I have to find the central routing circuitry."

"Spare us the details," Joe said. "Just hit a few circuits with a hammer, and I'm sure the phone system will start working like magic."

Phil ignored Joe's sarcasm. He poked around among the wires until he came to a metal box.

"This may help," he said. "I'll just open this door and"—the door of the box popped open—"and have a look around."

"What do you see?" Frank asked.

"Looks like this is what we're looking for," Phil said. "I'll just switch a couple of wires, and I think I can get one of the phones working."

"Good job!" Joe exclaimed.

Phil bustled around with the wires. Suddenly there was a sizzling sound. A bright shower of electric sparks sprayed out of Phil's hands. With a loud popping noise, Phil was blown right out of the small room, landing on his back next to Frank.

"Phil!" Frank shouted, crouching over his friend. "Are you all right?"

"Yeah," Phil said, his face contorted with pain. "Just got a bad shock. Haven't had that bad a shock since . . ."

"Since the last time you tried to fix Frank's computer?" Joe asked.

"That one was probably worse," Frank said. He turned to Phil. "Does this mean we won't be able to make a call out?"

"No, no," Phil protested. "I just have to be more careful."

Biff sniffed the air. "Hey, I think they're cooking something downstairs!"

Joe wrinkled his nose. "Whatever it is, I don't want to eat it. Smells like burning rubber."

"Uh-oh," Phil said, pointing into the telephone room. Black smoke started pouring out.

"Oh, no!" Joe cried. "You've set the room on fire!"

"And," Frank said, "we're locked in!"

12 Smoked Out

"Water!" Biff shouted. "We need water to put the fire out!"

"No, we don't," Phil said. "It's an electrical fire. It started when the wires began sparking. I think I caused a short circuit. What we need is sand to throw on the fire."

"Great," Joe said. "I'm sure we'll find whole dunes of sand in here."

"Maybe we can throw something else on it to smother it," Frank said.

Phil looked around. "Everything in here is flammable. There isn't even a rug."

Crackling flames could be seen inside the small room. It wouldn't be much longer before they reached the walls, which would go up like a tinderbox. And the smoke was getting thicker, making it difficult to breathe.

"My eyes feel like *they're* on fire," Joe said.

Loraleigh coughed. "My lungs are getting sore."

"Everybody get on the floor," Phil said. "The smoke will rise. We'll be able to breathe longer if we keep the smoke above our heads."

"Longer?" Joe asked. "What do we do when the whole room is full of smoke? Learn to breathe through old telephones?"

From outside the main door to the room a commotion could be heard. "What's going on in there?" Quentin's voice demanded.

"You know," Frank said quietly, "I think I'm actually glad to hear that guy's voice now."

The door burst open. Quentin poked his head inside angrily, the Brookburn brothers visible behind him.

"You're trying to burn the place down!" Quentin exclaimed. "You thought you could burn your way out of here, didn't you?"

"Er, not exactly," Joe said, then starting coughing.

"Go to the emergency supply closet and get a bucket of sand," Quentin said to the Brookburns. He waved a gun into the room. "The rest of you, get out of there. I can't see you in all that smoke."

Frank, Joe, and everybody else rushed gratefully past Quentin and into the hallway, a haze of black smoke following them. The Brookburn brothers came running back to the room, one of them with a bucket of sand in his hand and the other a fire extinguisher.

"Get that fire out fast," Quentin yelled at them. "With no fire department, we can't let it get out of control."

He turned the gun back on the Hardys and their friends. "I want you all to head downstairs. Bill McSavage will have a word with you."

As the Brookburn brothers worked to put out the fire, the rest marched back down the stairs they had come up twenty minutes earlier. McSavage was standing in the lobby, furious. He looked as if he was about to shout something angry, probably having to do with the fire, but Jack Mason beat him to it.

"We almost died up there, Bill!" he roared. "And I'm holding you personally responsible!"

"You idiot, Mason!" Bill roared back.

"Hey, don't you call my father an idiot!" Loraleigh shouted.

"Keep out of this, Loraleigh," Jack said. "This is between me and my old friend Bill."

"You were never my friend," McSavage said contemptuously. "You were always the goody-goody kid. You never liked working at the casino. I'm surprised you didn't turn us over to the police then. But now I'm going to take care of you. You and your goody-goody daughter. Like father, like daughter!"

To everyone's surprise, Jack Mason grabbed a vase off a table and ran toward Bill McSavage, smashing it over his head. McSavage, stunned, slumped to the floor.

Quentin rushed automatically toward him. Frank put out a leg, and the man tripped over it, falling to the wooden floor with a thud.

"Ha!" Biff said, waving one of his crutches in the air. "That'll take care of them!"

"Yeah," Joe said. "For about thirty seconds. Come on, everybody. Let's get out of here!"

Quite a parade poured out the front door of the McSavage mansion. Frank and Joe were in the lead, followed by Loraleigh and Jack Mason, Phil Cohen, and Biff bringing up the rear. Biff was limping along on crutches, but moving surprisingly fast with Rhonda at his side.

"Where to?" Joe asked. "Back to the trail?"

"No," Frank said. "They'll catch us there before we can go half a mile. We need a vehicle."

"The armored truck!" Joe said. "I noticed that the keys were still in the ignition."

"Perfect!" Frank said. "That way we can take the money out of town with us and hand it to the authorities."

They headed down the hill to the old barn, where Frank and Joe had earlier uncovered the truck. Once inside the barn, Joe barred the door, to keep any pursuers out.

"Okay," Frank said. "We have to work out seating arrangements. Phil, open the back door of the truck."

Phil pulled the door open, gaping at the sacks of money with astonishment.

"Now get inside," Frank continued. "Jack and Loraleigh, you can ride back there with Phil."

"What about me?" Rhonda asked.

"You ride up front with Joe and me," Frank said. "We'll need directions for getting out of town."

Phil, Jack, Loraleigh, and Biff crawled into the back. Phil pulled the door shut.

"Okay, who gets to drive?" Frank said.

"You go ahead," Joe said.

"Rhonda," Frank said, "climb in the middle."

"The cab on this truck looks pretty cramped," Rhonda said as she entered through the passenger side door, "but I may be able to squeeze in."

Once Rhonda was inside Frank jumped into the driver's seat and Joe into the passenger seat. Frank cranked the ignition. It made a sputtering noise, then roared to life.

"Looks like sitting under a pile of hay hasn't hurt it much," Joe said. "Sounds ready to go."

Frank shifted into gear and moved his right foot onto the accelerator.

"Um, shouldn't we open the barn door first?" Joe asked.

"Not on your life," Frank said. "Those guys may be waiting right outside. I don't want to give them any advance warning that we're on the way."

He floored the pedal and aimed the truck toward the bolted wooden doors. The vehicle bucked forward like a racehorse. Joe and Rhonda braced themselves against the dashboard.

The truck hit the door with a bang that could probably be heard all the way in town. The wooden bolt split in two, and the doors popped open. If anybody had been standing outside, the doors would have knocked them to the ground and put them out of the action for a while.

But nobody was waiting outside. Frank turned the truck up the hill, toward the main road leading from the mansion to Main Street. But coming down the hill toward the truck was a pair of motorcycles—and the Brookburn brothers were riding them.

"Uh-oh!" Joe said. "Maybe we'd better find another way out."

"They won't dare try to hit the truck," Frank said. "It would smash those bikes up pretty good."

"It might smash us up, too," Joe said. "Maybe we should go around in back of the house, over that way." He pointed to the right.

"No," Frank said. "Those guys will swerve first."

He continued driving straight up the hill, and the Brookburn brothers continued riding their bikes straight down. The truck whined as it negotiated the slope, but Frank put it in second gear and kept the accelerator floored.

"Maybe I should point out that I think those guys are crazy," Joe said.

The Brookburn brothers kept coming, straight toward the truck. Their eyes were glazed as though they didn't care if the truck hit them.

"Good point," Frank said, swerving to the right just before the Brookburn brothers struck them. Joe heaved a sigh of relief.

The Brookburn brothers obviously knew how to ride motorcycles, because they had turned and were on the tail of the truck within seconds. Frank drove toward the fields that Joe and the others had seen earlier.

"Just barrel on through," Rhonda said. "You're just driving through tall grass. You'll flatten it, but it won't slow you down too much."

"Or the motorcycles," Joe lamented.

"How come you know about driving through the fields?" Frank asked Rhonda.

"Let's just say I did some pretty crazy things when I was your age," Rhonda said.

"Probably not as crazy as getting into *this* situation," Joe said.

"Don't be so sure," Rhonda said.

They barely felt a bump as Frank plowed into the gently waving field of tall grass. He scanned the horizon for any sign of another way to get off Bill McSavage's farm but couldn't see one. Behind them, the Brookburn brothers plowed through the grass on their motorcycles, hard in pursuit.

"There's no other way out," Rhonda said. "You'll have to circle the mansion and head back to town."

"I was afraid of that," Frank said.

The mansion was on their left. Frank turned toward it, and the Brookburns turned with them. After a moment he was out of the field and riding across Bill McSavage's backyard.

"Okay," Joe said. "Just keep heading around the house and we'll be back on the road to town."

"Thanks," Frank said sarcastically. "You're better than a compass."

"Just trying to help," Joe said.

The front of the house came into view. Only a few hundred yards away was the road leading back through the main gates and into town.

Then something else came into view. A large old black limousine was blocking the road. Inside were Bill McSavage and Quentin.

13 Road Warriors

"We're trapped!" Joe shouted.

"No," Rhonda said. "Head for the fence. Over there!"

"Are you nuts?" Frank said. "We'll bounce off it!"

"There's a broken section," Rhonda said. "Just follow where I'm pointing."

Frank did as he was told, though he was reluctant to drive into the fence. The shrubbery on the other side looked pretty thick, too, but the truck just might be able to get through it.

The truck hit the fence and a large segment of it flew away, disappearing into the bushes. Then they hit a thick wall of green vegetation. There was a horrible crunching noise all around them as the truck snapped the branches of the shrubbery in front of them.

Then they were out the other side. Frank turned on the windshield wipers to knock off the branches that had become stuck to the window. Then he roared back onto the road and took it to Main Street.

"Okay, how do we get out of this town?" Frank asked.

"That way," Rhonda said, waving her hand. "The other end of Main Street."

Frank worried that they were leaving Chet all alone in this town, but knew his friend could ride Formby out. Frank had to save as many people as possible—they could come back for Chet later.

Frank headed in the direction that was definitely *not* toward the McSavage mansion. There was another short row of houses along the street, beyond which was a forest, not unlike the one on the other side of town where the path led back to the Appalachian Trail. The road entered the trees and Frank sped along it.

About a hundred feet into the forest the road forked.

"Which way do we go?" Frank asked.

"Maybe it doesn't make any difference," Joe said.

"No, it definitely makes a difference," Rhonda said. "Go that way," she said, pointing to the right. Frank thought he saw her hesitate briefly, but he followed her instructions.

The road was narrow and paved with gravel. Ruts

ran along through the trees where cars and trucks had driven for decades. The trees arched over them, forming a sort of canopy, making long and dark shadows.

There was a roar from behind them. Frank glanced in the sideview mirror. The Brookburn brothers were riding their cycles straight down the ruts in the road, right on their tail.

"It didn't take them long to catch up," Joe said.

"Probably took a shortcut," Frank said. "They guessed where we were headed."

"Well, they can't hurt us now," Joe crowed. "We'll be out of town in no time."

Even while Joe was saying those words, one of the two brothers pulled his motorcycle up alongside the truck, just outside Joe's window. He gave Joe a nasty look.

"Try to stop us now!" Joe yelled, returning the look.

"Don't encourage him," Frank said. "Those guys are still dangerous."

Sure enough, the motorcyclist raised a crowbar and swung it straight at Joe's window.

"Yow!" Joe cried, ducking. "That's not playing fair."

The crowbar hit the window hard but bounced off. The glass didn't break.

"Whew!" Joe said, relaxing again. "This thing has bulletproof glass. We're safe!"

105

"Don't get too comfortable," Frank said. "He can still do some damage with that thing."

The biker swung the crowbar again, this time at the hood of the truck.

"He's trying to get at the motor," Joe said. "You don't suppose he can break the hood open, do you?"

"I don't know," Frank said. "And I hope we get out of here before we find out."

A second blow from the crowbar set the hood vibrating. It looked as if it were about to pop open.

"I think I'd better get rid of this guy fast," Frank said, "before he causes serious damage."

Frank maneuvered the car toward the right side of the road, trying to cram the biker up against the trees. The motorcyclist saw what Frank was up to and put on his brakes, dropping behind the rear of the truck.

"Ha, that scared him away but good," Joe said, giving Frank the thumbs-up.

Suddenly there was a pounding noise from Frank's side of the truck. The other brother had pulled up on the left while Frank and Joe had been concentrating on the one to the right. He took a hard whack at the other side of the hood.

"They're double-teaming us!" Frank said.

Joe dug around under his seat. "Aha! I've found something that might help." He pulled out a crowbar like the ones the Brookburn brothers were using.

"Okay," Joe said to his brother. "Crowd the guy on

your side off the road so the other brother will pull up by my window."

"Whatever you say, little brother," Frank said.

Frank angled back to the left, and the biker on that side dropped behind the truck. Not surprisingly, the biker on the right pulled up again.

This time Joe was ready. He rapidly rolled down his window and held the crowbar outside. He gave the brother on his side a stiff whack across the chest.

"Oof," the biker sputtered as the air came rushing out of his lungs. His bike hit a tree, sending him spiraling into the woods. The bike itself bounced back and hit the truck, then toppled over.

The second Brookburn, behind the truck, didn't dodge in time. He hit his brother's overturned motorcycle at full speed and flipped head over heels, landing flat on the road.

"Ha!" Joe cried. "I don't think those guys will be bothering us again. They'll have headaches for a month."

"Yeah, well, let's worry about what's happening right now," Frank said. "How soon until we're off this gravel road and onto some real pavement, Rhonda?"

"Not long," Rhonda said. "There's a bridge not far ahead that leads out of town. Another mile or so past that, you'll hit the main highway."

"Yahoo!" Joe cried. "We're almost out of here!"

Frank turned around a bend. "There are a lot of

twists and turns in this road," he said. "It's almost like we're going in a circle."

"Look," Joe said. "Up ahead. I see a vehicle in the road. Maybe we can get help."

Frank felt a surge of hope, but it died almost immediately when he recognized the car.

It wasn't anybody who was likely to rescue them. It was the limousine with Bill McSavage and Quentin in it.

The Hardys and their friends really had gone in a circle. And now they were heading straight back to town!

14 A Bridge Too Far

Frank hit the brakes, but the truck skidded for another hundred feet on the gravel. Bill and Quentin stepped out of their car and smiled as the truck came to a stop. Quentin cocked his rifle for emphasis.

Another vehicle edged up beside the limo—a police car. It stopped and Sheriff Brickfield climbed out, patting his gun holster menacingly.

"And things were going so well there for a moment," Joe said with a sigh.

Sheriff Brickfield walked up next to Frank's window. "I think you boys had better step out of that vehicle. I'm going to have to arrest you for car theft."

Frank looked at him angrily as he opened the door. "Car theft? We weren't the ones who stole this truck. Bill McSavage and his friends stole it!"

"I don't know what you're talking about," Bill said. "I have no idea where that truck came from. Looked to me like you boys had it hidden away in my barn."

"*We* had it hidden away?" Joe shouted. "Boy, you've got a lot of nerve! Not only did you steal an armored truck full of millions of dollars in cash, but now you're blaming it on us? We were taking it to the authorities!"

"Save it for the jailhouse," Sheriff McSavage said. "Now, I hear you have some more folks with you. Are they hiding in the back?"

"Not hiding," Frank said. "Just going along for the ride."

Quentin walked to the back of the truck and opened the door. Phil Cohen came stumbling out on wobbly legs.

"Gee, do you think you guys could drive any worse?" he asked shakily. "I feel like I've been inside a blender for the last fifteen minutes." He noticed Quentin standing there with a rifle in his hands. "Wait a minute, what's this guy doing here? I thought we were getting out of town."

Jack Mason climbed out after Phil. "You again, Quentin?" he said. "I dislike you more every time I see you."

"The feeling is mutual," the man said with a smile.

Jack helped Loraleigh out of the truck. "Oh, no. We're still here," she said.

Biff pushed a crutch over the edge and used it to

leverage his way back to the ground. "At least we tried," he said.

"There's a jail right up the street. It's old but it does the trick," Sheriff Brickfield said. "I think we can all walk there. Even the kid on the crutches."

"But we didn't do anything," Joe said. "You must know *something* about what's going on in this town!"

"Oh, I'm sure he knows something about it," Frank said. "I bet you've been involved in this crime all along, haven't you, Sheriff?"

Sheriff Brickfield frowned. "Are you accusing me of being derelict in my duties as an officer of the law?" he asked.

"You bet I am!" Frank said.

"Remind me to throw away the key after I lock you up," the sheriff said, but he didn't seem particularly upset.

"You don't have to be shy, Paul," Bill McSavage said to Brickfield. "These boys already know so much that we might as well tell them the rest. Everybody in town that we could trust was part of the plan, and we're all splitting the cash from the robbery. Of course, there were a few people that we couldn't trust." He gave a meaningful glance at Jack and Rhonda.

"So what are you going to do with us now?" Jack asked. "Keep us locked up in jail forever? That jail isn't even big enough for all of us."

"It is if we cram you into the cells tight enough," Sheriff Brickfield growled.

"Besides," Bill said, "that's not really where we intend to keep you. We had planned to bury the truck after we had moved all the cash out of it. There's no reason we have to bury it empty."

"Does he mean what I think he means?" Biff asked.

"Yeah, I think he does," Frank said.

"You'll never get away with it," Joe proclaimed.

"If there's any justice in the universe," Jack Mason said, "I'll come back to haunt you for the rest of your life."

Bill snorted. "You've already haunted me since you left the casino. Trying to be my conscience."

"It was a dirty job," Jack said, "but somebody had to do it. Guess I didn't do it well enough."

"Insulting me to the last, Jack?" Bill said.

Joe noticed something out of the side of his eye while everyone else was watching the confrontation between Bill and Jack. Sheriff Brickfield had left the front door of his police car open, and there was an open pair of handcuffs on the floor in front of the driver's seat. Joe carefully edged around in back of the sheriff, dipped down as gracefully as he could, and picked up the cuffs. Then he edged away again.

Frank noticed what Joe was doing. He turned to the sheriff and said quietly, "You know, you really shouldn't leave a gun sitting on the front seat of your car like that."

The sheriff looked startled. "Gun? What gun?" He turned and rushed back to the car.

As quick as a magician pulling a scarf out of someone's ear, Joe grabbed the sheriff's right arm and snapped a cuff on his wrist. He snapped the other cuff to the outside of the car's window frame. Then he grabbed the sheriff's gun from its holster. Brickfield was taken totally by surprise.

"What did you just do to me?" he yelled, struggling in vain to get free.

"Get him out of those handcuffs!" Quentin commanded, aiming his rifle at Joe. "And drop that gun!"

Biff lunged forward, using one of his crutches as a lever, and tackled the servant in the midsection. Quentin and Biff fell to the ground in a tangle, the rifle flying from Quentin's hands. Meanwhile, Joe tossed the sheriff's gun to Jack Mason for safekeeping.

Bill McSavage's face turned red, and he started to yell something. But then he glanced at his car and realized that his own gun was still in the front seat. A look of fear crossed his face.

Jack Mason smiled. "Shoe's on the other foot now, Bill," he said. "Looks like you won't be burying us in that truck after all."

"You're not out of town yet," Bill said.

Jack turned to Joe. "Sheriff Brickfield should have

some more handcuffs in that car. Think you guys could grab a couple and put them on Bill and Quentin?"

"I'd be happy to." Joe beamed.

"Count me in," Frank added.

Biff rolled off Quentin. "Owww! I think I hurt my leg again!"

"It wasn't much fun having you land on top of me, either," Quentin said.

Rhonda knelt next to Biff. "You'll need medical attention, but it'll have to wait until we get out of town."

Biff grumbled but could hardly disagree. Being in pain seemed a lot less important than getting away from Morgan's Quarry.

Joe handcuffed Bill McSavage to one door of the old limousine while Frank handcuffed Quentin to another.

"Where are the keys to these things?" Frank said. "We'd better take them so these guys can't follow us again."

"Right there," Jack Mason said, pointing at Sheriff Brickfield's belt.

Joe grabbed for the keys, but Sheriff Brickfield swatted him with his free hand.

"Oh, no, you don't!" Frank said, grabbing the sheriff's arm in both of his hands. Joe unclipped the key chain and put it in his pocket.

"We're ready to go," Frank said, grabbing the sheriff's gun and Bill's and Quentin's rifles. "Everybody back in the truck."

"Can you promise to drive a little better this time?" Phil Cohen said, climbing into the back with the confiscated guns.

"I'll try," Frank said. "But the roads out of town are pretty bumpy."

Once everybody was in the back, Joe closed the doors. Then Frank, Rhonda, and Joe got into the cab. Frank revved up the engine and put the truck in gear.

"Okay," he said. "This time we'll take the left fork in the road."

"I'm really sorry about what happened," Rhonda said. "I leave this town so rarely that I actually forgot which road to take. Can you forgive me?"

"Of course," Joe said. "You've helped us out since we've been here. And you've been great to Biff."

Frank hit the accelerator and headed out of town again. This time, when they reached the fork in the road, he headed to the left.

The road was a little smoother, but the ride was still bumpy. Frank could have sworn he heard Phil Cohen yelling at him from the back of the truck, but through the armor he couldn't tell what was being said.

The trees opened into a clearing. A wooden structure loomed up ahead.

"The bridge?" Joe said.

"Yes, that's the bridge," Rhonda said.

"Then we're almost out of town," Frank said.

"You know," Joe said, "maybe you were right when you said we shouldn't get too excited before we're completely out of this place. I've got a bad feeling."

Frank slowed as he approached the bridge. It didn't look especially rickety, but it was obviously old and he wanted to cross it as slowly as possible. He eased the truck onto the wooden surface.

Each plank made a groaning noise as they passed over it, but the bridge seemed to be solid. Joe held his breath but was prepared to let it out in a sigh of relief.

Then everything seemed to spin in a circle in front of them. The bridge was tilting to the left. The truck slid to one side and hit the wooden guardrail, which snapped in two like the fence they had driven through earlier.

Then the truck fell off the bridge and plummeted toward a small stream below!

15 Stream of Unconsciousness

Frank awoke to the splash of cold water across his face. Where was he? He figured he must have lost consciousness for a while.

He was lying on his left side, a heavy weight on top of him. He turned his head to see both Rhonda and Joe lying on top of him. They were all in the cab of the truck, but it had been rotated ninety degrees. Water was flowing through every tiny crack in the vehicle.

"Hey, you guys!" Frank shouted, spitting water from his mouth as he spoke. "Get off me before I drown!"

"Huh?" Joe said. "What happened? Oh, yeah, we took a header on the bridge. Well, not a header exactly . . ."

117

"Just get off of me!" Frank shouted again. "And get out of this truck! Fast!"

Rhonda moaned. Joe reached up and opened the passenger side window, which was now directly above them. He pulled himself up on the edge of the window, then reached down to pull Rhonda up after him. Frank pushed from below as Rhonda groggily allowed them to drag her out of the truck.

The three of them crawled out of the window and jumped to the water below. The truck was lying on its side in the middle of a shallow stream about twenty feet wide.

"Now what do we do?" Joe said. "How are we going to get this truck out of here?"

"Let's get everybody out of the back first," Frank said, opening the rear door. Phil Cohen came tumbling out, landing in the water with a splash.

"I take back what I said," Phil groaned. "That was just mildly lousy driving before. *This* was really bad driving!"

Loraleigh and Jack clambered out after him. Biff took a little longer to maneuver. He was barely able to use the crutches now because he was in so much pain.

"What happened?" Loraleigh asked.

"Looks like the bridge finally collapsed from old age," Rhonda said.

"No," Jack Mason said. "It wasn't old age. Look over there."

He walked to the bridge. A large section in the middle had broken off and was tilting precariously to one side. At the points where it had broken away from the rest of the bridge the wood had a cleanly sawed look.

"Somebody deliberately cut the bridge so that nobody could get across it," Jack said. "Probably those Brookburn boys. They wanted to make sure there was no way you boys could leave town."

"So what are we going to do with the truck?" Joe asked again. "Pull it out of here by hand?"

"Maybe we should just walk to the highway," Frank suggested. "We can hitch a ride to the nearest town."

"No," Rhonda said. "That would take too long. By then Sheriff Brickfield will be out of those handcuffs and coming after us."

"That's true," Jack said. "Someone will notice him missing and will unlock the cuffs. They'll let Bill and Quentin go, too."

"Then we'll pull the truck out ourselves," Frank said. "Come on, everybody. If we all lift together, maybe we can get it upright so we can drive out of the water."

"I'd like to help, guys," Biff said, "but I'm afraid I'll have sit this one out." He limped to one bank of the river and sat on a large rock, laying his crutches beside him.

Everybody else gathered along the top of the truck and reached into the water, gripping the lower edge of the roof as tightly as possible. On Frank's command, they began to lift.

The truck began to budge. Little by little, as everybody strained, it rose slowly until it was about two feet out of the streambed. Then nobody could lift it any farther. Finally, their arms fatigued, the group eased the truck back into the stream.

"It's no use," Jack Mason said. "We'll never get this thing upright without help."

"Well, where are we going to find help in the middle of the woods?" Frank asked.

His question was answered by the sound of galloping hooves coming up the road from the town. Chet Morton appeared at the head of the collapsed bridge, atop the muscular horse from the farm.

"Hey, you guys tried to leave without me!" he yelled at the group.

"Sorry," Joe said. "We had to save the group, and you were impossible to find. I thought you were going to take that horse back to the barn hours ago."

"I wanted to, but Formby couldn't stand to be parted from me," Chet answered sheepishly. "So what are you trying to do? And why are you standing around in the middle of a river?"

"We're trying to get out of here," Frank said.

"People are trying to kill us," Joe added.

"And Mr. Lousy Driver here dumped our truck in the water," Phil Cohen said.

"People are trying to kill us?" Chet asked. "You mean those guys back on the road who are handcuffed to their cars? Boy, were they yelling at me when I rode past."

"Yeah, those guys," Joe said. "And some of their friends."

"So why don't you help us get the truck out?" Frank asked.

"Sure," Chet said, jumping off the horse and scrambling down the riverbank.

"Actually, it's the help of your horse that we'd like," Joe said.

Chet stopped and looked back up the slope. "Oh, yeah," he said. "Formby's pretty strong. He could probably get that truck right out of there."

Chet went back up and led the horse into the water. The cold stream didn't seem to bother Formby.

Jack Mason grabbed the ropes from off the bags of money, and Frank and Joe lashed three of them around the truck. Then they connected the other ends to Formby's harness. The horse stood calmly next to the truck, on the opposite side from the others.

"Now, everybody," Frank said, "we'll push while Formby pulls."

They stooped down and grabbed the roof of the truck. Chet mounted the horse and yelled, "Giddyap!"

All at once the horse began to strain against the ropes. The others began to lift as hard as they could. This time the truck began to rise more quickly out of the water: one foot, two feet, three feet . . .

Finally, with an extra burst of effort, the truck was out of the water and standing on its wheels again. Everyone cheered.

"Let's see if it works," Frank said, jumping into the cab. The ignition made a rumbling sound, but the engine wouldn't turn over.

"It must be flooded," Joe said.

"Literally," Phil added.

"Floor it, Frank," Joe said. "That'll get gasoline back into the engine."

"That's what I'm doing," Frank replied.

Finally the engine did turn over and roar to life. Everybody cheered.

Rhonda walked up to Frank's side of the cab, where the door was still open. She reached inside and, before Frank was aware of what she was doing, turned the engine off and pulled the keys out of the ignition. She clutched them tightly in one hand and threw them far off into the bushes.

"Hey, what was that about?" Frank yelled, startled.

"Yeah," Joe said. "We were almost out of here. For real, this time."

"Sorry, guys," she said, pulling a gun from the pocket of her pants. "You're not going anywhere. We're waiting here for Bill McSavage and Sheriff Brickfield—and then you're all going back to Morgan's Quarry, where you belong."

16 A Friend in Need

Frank desperately looked around for the guns they had taken from the sheriff and the others. Then he saw them—underwater and useless.

Biff grabbed his crutches and pulled himself to his feet.

"Rhonda!" he exclaimed. "What are you talking about? You're supposed to be on our side!"

"The key phrase there is 'supposed to be,' " Rhonda said cryptically. "Unfortunately, you 'supposed' wrong. I was in on the plans for the robbery from the very beginning. In fact, I'm the one who suggested it, after I found out that the Brookburn boys knew somebody who drove an armored truck for a large bank."

"Then . . . then why have you been helping us?" Frank asked.

"You brought me someone who was injured," Rhonda said. "I'm a nurse. I swore a long time ago to heal the wounded, and that's what I did."

"But why did you pretend to help us escape?" Joe asked. "Why were you locked in that room with Biff back at the McSavage mansion?"

"Bill McSavage came to me before you even arrived at my house," Rhonda said. "He told me what had happened, that you boys had seen the money, and that I should pretend to be on your side so I could keep my eyes on you in case you tried to get out of town."

"I don't believe this," Biff said. "I really thought we were friends."

"I . . . I was just pretending," Rhonda said, looking away from Biff as she spoke. "It was all a ruse, you understand. Just a ruse to keep you in town."

"No, it wasn't," Biff said. "I really enjoyed chatting with you."

"Well, I like telling old war stories," Rhonda said. "Hard to shut me up some times. That's all."

Joe cleared his throat loudly. The others turned toward him, expectantly. A conspiratorial smile crossed his face.

"Hey, Rhonda!" he said. "You didn't think we were actually going to turn this money over to the police, did you? We just said that because we thought you wouldn't help us otherwise. Frank and I were going to ditch you, take the money, and split it with our friends. Isn't that right, guys?"

Slowly Frank and Phil nodded agreement. Even Jack and Loraleigh joined in, though reluctantly. Only Biff seemed oblivious to Joe's scheme. He kept staring at Rhonda.

"But now that we know you were in on the scheme," Joe went on, "we'll split it with you, too. In fact, since you were the mastermind, we'll give you half. I bet your friends back in town wouldn't let you have that much. Now they'll be cut out completely. And they can't go to the authorities because they'd all end up in jail for aiding and abetting."

"I don't believe you," Rhonda said. "You seem like a nice bunch of kids. You wouldn't get involved in anything like that."

"You seem pretty nice, too," Joe said. "But, hey, it turns out that you're as scuzzy as the rest of us."

"So are you inviting me to come with you?" she asked. "And split the money when we get out of town?"

"You bet," Joe said. "We're all friends here. And friends share things with their friends, right?"

"Uh, yeah," Phil Cohen said unenthusiastically.

"Sure thing," Frank added.

"So how about it?" Joe said. "Why don't you put that gun away and hop back in the truck. We'll be out of this stream in no time."

"Good thing," Phil said. "My feet are about to freeze off."

Rhonda pondered Joe's remarks. "No," she said finally. "I can't do it. I can't betray my friends. We're going to wait for them to arrive."

"I'm your friend, too," Biff said. "I know I am. How can you betray *me*?"

He moved forward, but one of the wet crutches slipped abruptly from his grasp. As his injured foot touched the ground, he let out a yelp and collapsed.

Rhonda acted instinctively, rushing to help him. Joe reacted just as quickly, running up behind her and grabbing her gun. Rhonda barely seemed to notice, so intent was she on helping Biff.

"That was a dirty trick," Rhonda muttered to Biff.

"It wasn't a trick," Biff said. "I really fell."

"Why don't you hang on to this," Joe said, handing the gun to Jack Mason. "I don't think we'll be needing it anymore."

Brighton wasn't large, but it looked like a major metropolitan area compared to Morgan's Quarry. It had a police station run by competent officers. It also had a small but well-staffed hospital, where Frank and Joe sat near the emergency room, waiting for the doctor to report on Biff's condition. It was late evening and they were extremely tired, but they wanted to find out how Biff was doing before they checked into the local motel. Jack and Loraleigh sat across from them, as Phil Cohen played with a piece of high-tech medical equipment. Chet was off somewhere looking for the snack room.

"Hey, this is a pretty nice piece of equipment!" Phil said, examining a video monitor that could display a patient's heart rate, blood oxygen level, and several dozen other things. It wasn't hooked up to a patient at the moment, so the colored lines that ran from one side of the screen to the other were all flat.

"Couldn't be *too* good," Joe said. "The patient seems to be dead."

Phil gave him a dirty look. Jack Mason stood up and walked across to the Hardys.

"I want to thank you boys again for helping us," he said.

"Thank us?" Frank asked. "We're the ones who ought to be thanking you. You and Loraleigh helped us get out of Morgan's Quarry alive."

"We didn't help out that much," Jack said. "But you boys got me to do what I should have done a long time ago: confront Bill McSavage and get him to shut down his illegal operations."

"Well, you didn't know he *had* any illegal operations anymore," Joe said.

"True," Jack said. "But there were all those years when he ran the casino. And I should have known he'd be up to something again."

"I can't tell you how glad I am to be out of that town," Loraleigh said. "I've spent my entire life in Morgan's Quarry, but there are so many people there who frightened me. Like those Brookburn brothers. And I never really liked Bill McSavage, even though he was our biggest customer. There was something evil behind his eyes, even when he was laughing and smiling."

"So where will you and your father be going now?" Frank asked.

"To relatives," Jack Mason said. "We'll move in with them for a while. Then we'll start a new life, a long way from Morgan's Quarry."

Just then an imposing white-haired figure appeared in the door to the emergency room. It was Ron Hansen, police chief of Brighton. The Hardys had met him earlier when they arrived in town with the truck full of cash. They hadn't wanted to spend any more time hauling the stolen loot around than they had to.

"Thought you fellas would like to know," he said. "Bill McSavage and friends have been picked up over in Morgan's Quarry and are on their way here for questioning."

"All right!" Joe said, applauding. "I hope you throw the book at him."

"Even better," Chief Hansen said. "The FBI is coming to town. Turns out that the money was taken over state lines, so now it's a federal case. Mr. McSavage is probably going to spend the rest of his life in jail."

"Where he belongs," Jack said.

"Looks like the Hardy Boys have solved another case," Joe said, leaning back and putting his hands behind his head. There was a smug look on his face.

"With a little help from our friends," Frank said, gesturing toward Jack, Loraleigh, Phil, and Chet, who had just returned with several bags of snacks and two hot dogs.

"Speaking of your friends," Chief Hansen asked, "how's that Biff fella doing?"

"There's the man you should ask," Joe said, pointing to a youngish doctor in a white coat who was standing at the edge of the crowd, not wanting to interrupt the conversation.

"Why, hello, Dr. Mitchell," Chief Hansen said. "I should have known you'd be the one taking care of Biff."

The doctor nodded shyly. "Anyway, I wanted everybody to know that Biff's okay."

"Thank goodness," Frank said. "How's his leg doing?"

"Pretty well," the doctor said, "considering what he's been through. He'll be off it for six weeks, and it'll be at least two months before he can play football again, but he shouldn't have any lasting problems."

"That's good news," Chet said. "All of Bayport

High would be in mourning if we lost our best full-back."

"So I guess this means we can go back to the Appalachian Trail and pick up where we left off," Phil said excitedly.

Frank, Joe, and Chet all swiveled their heads toward their friend, giving him their most withering looks.

"You'll be hiking alone," Joe said. "I don't want to be near a trail again for a good long time."

"Or until we have another case," Frank said, "to make you forget about this one."

"Which should be just about any time," Chet said. "You guys have a knack for finding trouble."

"Well, don't lose the knack," Jack Mason said. "If you can help other people like you helped us, you should keep right on finding trouble."

"I think," Frank said quite sincerely, "that's one thing that Joe and I can guarantee."

CAROLYN KEENE
NANCY DREW
GIRL DETECTIVE

Secret Sabotage

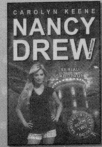

Serial Sabotage

Sabotage Surrender

Secret Identity

Identity Theft

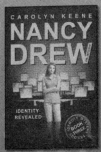

Identity Revealed

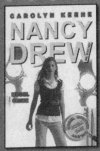

Model Crime

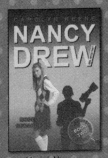

Model Menace

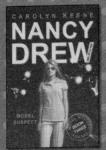

Model Suspect

INVESTIGATE THESE THREE THRILLING MYSTERY TRILOGIES!

Exciting fiction from three-time Newbery Honor author Gary Paulsen

Newbery Honor Book

Newbery Honor Book

Aladdin Paperbacks and Simon Pulse
Simon & Schuster Children's Publishing
www.SimonSays.com